PRAISE FOR
DATING BIG BIRD

"Laura Zigman, author of last year's bestseller *Animal Husbandry,* has topped herself with this wry novel."
—*WOMAN'S OWN*

"Full of wit and charm and insight . . . You will be rooting all the way for Ellen Franck in this delicious book." —*NEWSDAY*

"Funny and convincing enough to penetrate the cynicism of readers who still associate parenthood with 'minivans and portacribs.'" —*USA TODAY*

"The thirty-five-year-old narrator of Laura Zigman's second novel is undeniably likable . . . she'd be fun to have drinks with."
—*THE NEW YORK TIMES*

"A tale that makes for laughs and touching moments . . . well told and funny." —*KIRKUS REVIEWS*

"The absorbing train of events and amusing dialogue make this a lark of a read." —*PUBLISHERS WEEKLY*

"Charming, witty . . . an amusing fairy tale." —*BOOKPAGE*

"A light, breezy read, enjoyable."
—*THE WALL STREET JOURNAL*

"Often hilarious . . . [A] clever, zippy new novel."
—*THE DETROIT NEWS/FREE PRESS*

"As you read, you'll laugh yourself into imaginary labor pains, but you also cringe at the poignancy between the lines."
—*THE NASHVILLE TENNESSEAN*

D A T I N G

B I G

B I R D

. . . .

L A U R A   Z I G M A N

D E L T A   T R A D E   P A P E R B A C K S

A Delta Book
Published by
Dell Publishing
A division of Random House, Inc.
1540 Broadway
New York, New York 10036

For information, address Dell Publishing, New York, New York.

Delta® is a registered trademark of Random House, Inc., and the colophon is
a trademark of Random House, Inc.

ISBN: 0-385-33341-2

Reprinted by arrangement with The Dial Press, a division of
Random House, Inc.

Book design by JoAnne Metsch

Manufactured in the United States of America

Published simultaneously in Canada

February 2001

10 9 8 7 6 5 4 3 2 1

BVG

For Jenny Loviglio,

for Marian Brown,

and for Nicole and Michael,
my Pickle and my Monkey

THE

FIRST

TRIMESTER

1

. . .

IT'S NOT THAT I found Big Bird particularly attractive, it's
just that I thought he would make a good parent.

I mean *father.*

Parent implied an extended relationship I wasn't necessarily banking on.

Not that I wouldn't have wanted an extended relationship. It's just that I was trying to be realistic. I was thirty-five,
after all, and by then I knew the difference between expecta-
tion and desire; between love and lust; between boyfriends
and fathers.

At least, I was supposed to know.

Contemplating impregnation by an eight-foot yellow
bird is just one example of how carried away you can get
when you want a child as much as I did.

You have to admit, though, that except for the feathers—
and the horizontally striped tights, and the bulging eyes, and
that stupid pointy beak—Big Bird would be the ideal parent:

He's warm.

He's affectionate.

He's had a stable job for almost as long as I can remember.

And you'd always know where to find him in case you needed anything later on.

Giving birth to a baby covered in a fuzzy down of yellow feathers would be a small price to pay for such exemplary paternal qualities.

My friend Amy, though, preferred Barney. She would cite his trademark song as evidence of his superior genes:

♩♪ *I love you. You love me. We're a happy family . . .* ♩♪ ♩♪

But when I'd point out how a happy family might be beyond our reach but a child wasn't—she'd reluctantly agree.

Then she'd confess the true reason for her preference:

She liked purple better than yellow.

TELLING PEOPLE YOU want to have kids when you're not married doesn't exactly go over like *The Red Balloon*. It's not like everyone you know—parents, married friends, single friends, boyfriends—will be waiting in your own personal receiving line after some wedding or baby shower to congratulate you on having a few too many vodka martinis and transforming yourself into their vision of the living breathing female cliché.

But for once, you're not feeling like a cliché.

For once, you're not bemoaning your unmarried barren state.

Despite the fact that you are, quite obviously, drunk, you're in surprisingly good spirits.

In fact, you're feeling rather empowered.

Publicly expressing your desire to have a child is the first step to achieving it.

OBVIOUSLY I UNDERSTOOD that I would need to prepare for such a radical addition to my life—to feather my nest, as it were.

First, I would need a bigger apartment to make room for a crib.

And a changing table.

And a Diaper Genie.

Two, I would need the crib.

And the changing table.

And the Diaper Genie.

Three, I would need more money.

So I could afford the bigger apartment.

And the nursery equipment.

Not to mention the nanny, since I'd have to keep working to pay for it all.

"Aren't you forgetting something?" Amy would ask.

I'd stare at her blankly.

Crib.

Changing table.

Diaper Genie.

Bigger apartment.

Nanny.

More money.

And then it would dawn on me.

"A stroller."

"I see," she'd say, doubling over and slapping her leg. "So you're still planning on reproducing asexually."

FOR A WHILE, I wasn't planning on reproducing at all. I thought I might just kidnap my niece and spare myself all the trouble and aggravation:

Why risk having a child you might not like when there's already an existing child you adore?

At first, my older sister, Lynn, was entertained by such displays of my passionate aunthood. Then, as the first year passed and moved into the second, and Nicole—"the

Pickle"—became more and more of an animal, Lynn began to really latch on to the idea.

"You can have her," she'd say, staring at the floor where the screeching wailing flailing fit-throwing beast-in-a-diaper had thrown herself down in protest over an enforced nap.

But each display of histrionics only made me covet her more.

She's an animal, I'd swoon. *But she's* my *animal.*

NOT THAT I really considered stealing her. I just liked to borrow her sometimes. Take the baby-idea out for a little reality test-drive when I went to visit her.

Pushing the stroller through the park, taking her for a ride in the family Jeep, dragging her kicking and screaming through the supermarket when she should have been eating or napping, I'd beam at passersby with the pride and bliss of a new mother.

"She's got her father's temperament," I'd say, and shrug blamelessly.

Which was true.

My brother-in-law always gets cranky when he's hungry and tired.

IT WAS THE Pickle who first opened the door to the possi-bilities of Big Bird as a husband and father and made me wonder whether I should, in my next relationship (if I ever had a next relationship), consider going against type (tall, dark, and withholding) in favor of something new and dif-ferent (yellow, feathered, and friendly).

She and Lynn and my brother-in-law Paul had driven down from Maine to New York that Labor Day weekend for a wedding at the Waldorf, and the Saturday afternoon before the ceremony they brought her downtown to my apartment on West Thirteenth Street for her sleepover. I'd spent weeks preparing for our big night together, and before they all arrived, I checked my weekend inventory one last time.

M&M's.

Waffles.

Library books.

Barney, Blue's Clues, and *Teletubbies* videotapes.

A pair of platform sneakers and a pair of fuzzy *Cat in the Hat* slippers wrapped inside their Payless boxes.

And three dresses from Baby Gap.

Lynn came up first while Paul parked the car with Nicole.

"I have to pee this minute or I'm going to explode," she said, the desperation rising in her voice. "I'm starting to think I should wear those adult diapers because I never get to go." She gave me a quick peck on the cheek before dropping the pile of bedding and clothing and Barbie dolls and teddy bears that she'd brought up from the car on the couch in the living room. She headed toward the foyer, stopped short, then turned back to me in confusion. "Where's the—?"

"The potty?" I pointed behind her to the little hallway on the opposite end of the little foyer. "It's that way."

I followed her—forever the younger sister, trailing behind—to the bathroom door, which she left partially open. I heard the seat cover go up, then a sigh of relief.

"You can come in," she said through the open door. "Everyone else does. I have no modesty left. In fact, I wonder if I can still pee when no one's watching me. I've probably developed some pathological need to go to the bathroom in front of people."

When she'd finished flushing and washing her hands, she came back out. Her jeans were still unzipped, and I could see

the elastic band of her underwear just below her belly button as we walked back together to the living room. "I'm
sorry," she said, starting to zipper herself before changing her
mind again. "I haven't worn these pants in months, but
they're still tight. I thought eight hours in the car might
stretch them out, but clearly I was wrong."

"You look great," I said with enough enthusiasm to make
her think I was lying, even though I wasn't. Her hair was shiny
and black and straight to her shoulders, and she'd always had a
great smile, which together almost completely distracted from
the toddler-induced dark circles under her eyes.

Lynn rolled her eyes. "I do not," she countered. "I'm a tub."

"You are not."

"I am, too."

"I can see you're as ill as you've always been," I said, finishing the same exchange we have whenever we see each
other again. It was our version of two apes preening each
other: *You look good. No,* you *look good. No* YOU *look good.*
Even though she was heavier since she'd had Nicole—a little extra padding on the hips and thighs—she was still far
from fat. She'd just been spoiled all her life. Being born
with an enviably long waist and a flat stomach that
required no maintenance of abdominal crunches will do
that to you.

She looked at me and grinned. The last time we'd seen each
other was two months ago—in early July, when I managed to
eke out a week's vacation with them and my parents on Cape
Cod. "Your hair's gotten so long," she said. "And straight."

"Like yours."

People always said we looked like twins, but Lynn and I
had never seen the strong resemblance. Just coloring—
brown eyes and olive skin—and hairstyle, if I grew mine out
and blow-dried the hell out of it.

"Well, you look great. How's . . . ?"

Malcolm? "He's fine. He's the same." Which is what I always said when she asked and which meant: *Don't ask. I don't want to talk about it.*

"Maybe someday we'll meet him."

"Maybe." I doubted it.

And just as I was starting to wonder what was taking Paul and the Pickle so long to come up from the garage, Lynn and I heard a howling screech that Dopplered from the elevator in the hallway, past my door, and then back to it as they finally located the correct apartment. With excitement and dread—My Pickle was here! But she was not happy!—I lunged for the doorknob and saw Paul, wrestling back arms and legs and miniature Timberland-booted feet as he failed miserably to maintain some semblance of control over his daughter.

Nicole was adorable in thick white textured tights, miniature red plaid kilt, and denim jacket. In between her wild writhings and through all the tears and sniffling, I could see her baby teeth: the two front ones on top pushed out from too much pacifier sucking. It seemed every time I saw her now, she had either just cried, was just about to cry, or was indeed crying, and at that very moment she was somewhere in between all three stages. I saw her eyes register me, but my fantasy that that would be enough to stop her tantrum was ill-conceived and short-lived.

"Hiiiiiiiyyyyy!" I squealed, bending down and opening my arms for the big greeting, but Paul pushed past me without bothering to say hello. Not that I blamed him, of course. The Pickle's unwieldy fluff of curly brown hair was, after all, covering his mouth at the time, and she had just hit him twice on the side of the head with her Madeline doll.

"It was the M&Ms," he said, as he bent down and lowered her onto the kilim rug. He looked like he'd just stepped out of the L.L. Bean catalog with his multiple layers of turtle-neck and sweater and zippered fleece jacket, even though here in New York, three hundred miles south of the Maine tundra, it was still summer. "She wanted more than the five we gave her."

"When we said no—" Lynn added, playing couple's tag-team storytelling and setting Paul up for his next line.

"She flipped out."

"She hates it when—"

"—we say no."

"Or anything that—"

"—rhymes with no."

They looked at each other with bemused frustration and exhaustion. Paul's wire-rimmed glasses were askew on his nose, and Lynn still hadn't zipped up her pants—while I—the uninitiated, the unprepared, the inexperienced guest-host aunt who was suddenly wondering whether she should have added a leash and muzzle to her list of sleep-over supplies—simply watched the epic unraveling continue: the final slow-motion meltdown as Nicole flung herself flat onto the floor, head back first with a sickening thud, eyes to the heavens, screaming bloody murder.

For a few seconds, we all stared down at the rug, shaking our heads and wondering, I was sure, the same exact thing: *How can something so small and so cute make so much noise?* Then Paul bent down, then Lynn bent down, then I bent down—all three of us baby-talking and crawling around on the floor in the hopes of cajoling her back to civility. But given the fact that she was understandably tired and cranky from the long drive and not used to my apartment yet, the crying continued.

"Any change in her daily routine is very disruptive," Lynn said. "She hates change."

"Me, too," I said.

Paul caught Lynn's eye to signal that it was time for them to leave, though I doubted they actually needed five hours to get dressed for the wedding.

"You're sure you really want one?" they said in unison while standing in the doorway. They were looking at me as if I were a madwoman.

Speechless, frozen-smiled, briefly glancing over my shoulder at the rug in my foyer, wondering when and if this tantrum would ever cease—I nodded unconvincingly.

Of course I did.

Didn't I?

But once I administered the recommended remedy for a code one tantrum—two Fig Newtons with a chaser of five M&M's—and the screaming had stopped; once they each kissed Nicole good-bye and finally slid out the door and I'd picked her up off the floor and wiped her tear-stained face with the bottom half of my white T-shirt; once it was just the two of us alone in the precious silence of the late afternoon Labor Day weekend—her drying her eyes and holding my hand as she walked shyly into the kitchen and the bedroom and back into the hallway toward the living room—once she'd opened her presents and put her new *Cat in the Hat* slippers on her hands like puppets and tried to shove them in my mouth; once I knew what it felt like to be her only focus—what it felt like to feel just right—I reconsidered their question.

Yes, I did want my own Pickle.

I knew it.

I was sure of it.

IN THE BLISSFULLY quiet posttantrum hours, Nicole and I ate a box of Eggo waffles (hers cut into eight pieces—not seven, or six, or nine, but eight exactly) while watching

Barney videotapes and coloring in coloring books. Then she went into my bedroom closet and tried on all my shoes, falling over several times before finally returning to her own favorite pair of bejeweled Barbie dress-up mules, which she slipped on and pranced around the room in. Mesmerized and barely able to breathe at the sight of her—all diaper and three-year-old chubby legs clip-clopping back and forth across the room—the vision of me when I was her age, if family photos and lore about my legendary baby-fat and predisposition for theatrical nudity were any indication—I finally grabbed her by the back of her Pampers and pulled her up onto the bed with me.

"You . . . are . . . my . . . Pickle!" I said, my face so close to hers, she became a giggling blur of fluffy hair and baby teeth.

"No way!" She grabbed my nose with one hand and tried to stick the fingers of her other hand into my mouth.

"Yes way!"

"No way! I'm not a pickle. I'm Nicole."

I grabbed her cheeks and put my face up against hers. "Okay, then: *Nose kiss!*" I yelled.

"Nose kiss!" she yelled back.

We were both laughing so hard that before the one of us not wearing the diaper peed by accident, I reached for the book she'd picked out for me to read—*Curious George Goes to the Hospital*—and opened it up. Exhausted, we curled up next to each other as we turned the pages—me, for once, thinking only of my delight in her being there and not about how, in less than twelve hours, her perfect smooth chubby baby-flesh would be gone. But it didn't take long before Nicole became distracted, restless—I was never quite sure if she actually listened to the stories when I read them to her or if she just enjoyed soaking up the attention of being read to—pushing the book away and sitting up to ask me a seemingly urgent question.

"Where's your hud-band?"

I blinked. "My hud-band? I don't have a hud-band," I said without shame and with just enough lilt in my voice to even suggest pride.

"Do you have a Big Bird?"

"You mean, like, a boyfriend?"

She nodded.

I blinked several times.

Kind of.

Sort of.

In a manner of speaking.

It depended on how you defined boyfriend.

"No."

Her forehead grew furrowed.

"Do you have a Elmo?"

Ditto my forehead.

"No."

"Do you have . . . a Barney?"

"No."

"Do you have . . . a Mickey Mouse?"

"No."

"Do you have . . . Teletubbies?"

She stared at me, then shrugged her shoulders with her arms outstretched at her sides.

"Then *what* do you *have*?"

"I have nothing," I exhaled, now thoroughly deflated and humiliated, not only by the naked horror of the word that had seeped out of my mouth but by the look in the Pickle's eyes when I'd uttered it:

Pity.

"Auntie LaLa needs something to have."

And before I knew it, she was climbing down out of the bed and heading over to the pile of stuffed animals Lynn had brought with them. When she turned back to me and handed me her Big Bird, it was with a child's absolute conviction that loneliness and sadness could be made to disappear—just like that.

"Big Bird," she said, "to sleep with Auntie LaLa."

2

. . .

I DID NOT always want to have a child.

For a while, the idea of procreating and reproducing and all that came with it was completely unappealing:

The stretch marks and weight gain and exhaustion and complete lack of privacy. And freedom. And time.

The mysterious pod-person personality-replacement that transformed previously normal women into Spalding Gray–type monologuists, carrying on at cocktail parties or in supermarket aisles about vaginas and episiotomies and effluvia of every sort and variation without any visible signs of embarrassment. Or irony. Or stopping.

The Jeeps and minivans and Portacribs and strollers and enormous shoulder-strapped survival bags stuffed with toys and dolls and stickers and puzzles and hundreds of little Ziploc Baggies filled with every imaginable contingency cereal and cookie and candy and fruit to prevent—or at least contain—public tantrums since all the new parenting theories seemed to denounce the previously accepted concept of *no*.

The desire to recognize traces of myself in a child's face, to be reflected in a child's eyes—to be reached for, cried for, needed at all times of the day and night—did not haunt me— did not occur to me, even—until three years ago. Before then, my vision of love and absolute connection and bliss—a man and me, frozen in time and space, in mid-breath, in mid-sentence, in mid-kiss—had always been the same.

My vision had never included a baby.

Or was the baby.

With or without a Big Bird.

That vision took longer to appear.

It took until I grew tired of myself and wished for the relief of distraction.

It took until the nights became too quiet and too lonely to bear.

It took until I laid eyes on my niece.

That's when I knew.

When I knew I didn't want to live without one.

NOTHING HAD PREPARED me for what I would feel for her, that enormous wave of rapture that came over me the first time I laid eyes on her right after she was born.

Paul had called me at three in the morning from the hospital pay phone to give me the news, and while I was excited to be a first-time aunt, I had no idea that my life would be so completely changed.

What it was about her that captured me so, I'll never know, since she had a big head and no hair and looked far more like my brother-in-law than my sister—or me—she had a round face instead of a long and narrow one; blue eyes instead of brown; white skin instead of olive—but capture me she did, right then and right there, that first time when I lifted her out of my sister's arms and carefully draped her over my shoulder and felt her short shallow breath on the side of my neck.

Maybe it was because I finally had someone I could lavish attention on and love without restriction.

Or maybe it was simply the benign narcissistic thrill of being part of a child's growing consciousness, of feeling that you are becoming and will remain a permanent fixture in their universe. Of needing to affect someone, to make a difference in someone's life, to prevent the secret wound of loneliness and sadness from ever existing in them the way it exists in you. Whatever it was, my attachment to her became a certainty that grew stronger with every visit—as sitting and crawling turned to cruising and walking—as the gurgling sounds and monosyllables over the phone once a week turned into words and half sentences and little conversations and then, even, my name—albeit her version of it—I knew, with a sureness I had felt about little else in my life, that I would have to have my own child someday, some way, somehow.

Because for those three or four or five days every few months when we saw each other, my Pickle and I would be inseparable.

We'd eat together.

Read stories together.

Sleep together.

And wake up early together.

Behavior completely befitting two people in love.

SINCE IT'S HARDER to be left than to be the one leaving, it was always worse for me when Lynn, Paul, and Nicole left after a visit, and the Waldorf wedding weekend was no exception. The quiet; the order; the overwhelming stillness where there had just been so much chaos and noise and movement was what I dreaded most.

Paul would want to be on the road by eight A.M., so I always took precautions the night before her departure to remove any reminders of the Pickle's presence from my apartment: After she'd go to sleep, I'd put the books that we'd read over and over and over—*Curious George, Stone Soup, Amelia Bedelia, Make Way for Ducklings*—back on the shelf; I'd melt the red Jell-O down the sink and rinse out the bowl; I'd sweep the floor clean of cereal and cookie crumbs and M&M's. That way, when I closed the door behind them, it was easier to pretend she had never been there at all. But there was always something left behind—a sock; a lollypop wrapper; a Cheerio stuck to the floor that I'd somehow missed; or the smell of soap and baby shampoo on my sheets and pillowcases, which I could hardly bear to launder away.

And when they'd gone—when the car had pulled out of the parking garage across from my building and driven slowly down the street and turned onto Sixth Avenue; when I'd stood long enough on the sidewalk with my palms pressed into my eyes to stop the tears and to keep the picture of her in my mind for as long as possible—her waving good-bye from her car seat and her hair, dark and curly and uncombed and wild just visible in the window—I'd come back in to my apartment, where the inescapable silence and solitude would overtake me, and where the traces of her always reemerged as if in high relief, like the sticky hand-print on the living-room window did where she'd had her time-outs that visit.

Then I would sit and stare into the empty space, completely and utterly alone, and I'd consider the increasingly urgent question of how I was going to get my own Pickle.

IF THERE WERE one thing I could do besides having a baby and besides coming to see that the way my life has turned out really isn't all that bad and is, in fact, even pretty good most times—it would be this:

To eradicate from the face of the earth all traces of the phrase *biological clock*.

I hate this phrase.

Not only is it annoyingly overused and pejorative, but it is stupid and incorrect.

Late at night, when I lie awake in the dark, wondering how I got to wherever it is I've gotten to, the image of a huge Big Ben clock ticking away my childbearing years is not the first one that comes to mind.

At least, not to my mind, anyway.

This is what comes to my mind:

A gum-ball machine.

Dispensing its limited supply of eggs.

One by one.

Month after month.

Year after year.

Egg.

Egg.

Egg.

3

. . .

A WEEK AFTER the Pickle had left, I walked up University Place on Sunday morning on the way to the office to put a few hours of work in before my nightmarish week ahead. "Fashion Week"—when New York was transformed even more into Style Ground Zero than it already was by bringing in designers and models and scary thin rich people from around the world for shows and benefits and cocktail parties and dinners—was less than forty-eight hours away. As one of the many behind-the-scenes industry slaves, I had a million things to do; most of which—or all of which—had to do with making sure nothing went wrong.

Please.

Like it mattered now.

The day before, a three-year-old had, in so many words, pointed out that I had nothing.

No Barney.

No Elmo.

No Teletubbies.

Just a relationship with an older Big Bird (by almost

twenty years), who was complicated (divorced, depressed, despondent), difficult to explain (we slept together but didn't *sleep* together), and whom I'll get to later.

And a big job working for a big designer.

The job: Director of marketing, Karen Lipps New York.

The designer: Five foot five. One hundred and seventy-two pounds. Easily a size sixteen if she weren't a clothing designer and couldn't sew her own size-six labels into whatever she wore.

Karen Lipps was only ten years older than I, but she had a multigazillion-dollar company that had just gone public; four homes and another under contract; a husband; and a little girl, Marissa, two years old.

The latter of which was why she wasn't as thin as she used to be.

"She's not as thin as she used to be, ever since she had . . . *the child,*" her fawning but slightly evil British Uriah Heep–like assistant, Simon Marder, once whispered to me upon exiting a meeting. Karen had been particularly harsh about a pant sample that made the model look like she'd actually eaten in the past three weeks, and she had thrown a peeled banana at Annette, who oversaw the sample seam-stresses. Whenever Karen threw food or anything else at someone, Simon felt it was his responsibility—and perhaps his one opportunity to get a word in edgewise all day—to deconstruct her pathology to anyone who would listen.

"It drives her absolutely mad when the clothes don't lie completely flat against the body or if there's even the slightest bit of puckering," he continued in his hushed tone. "She considers it an injustice: *the illusion of fat where there really isn't any.*" He paused then and tucked his straight chin-length hair neatly behind his ears. "She hates fat, you see. Because she hates *being* fat. Not that she'd ever admit to it, poor thing. In her mind she's still a size four."

"Try telling her pants that," I suggested.

"Believe me, I've tried," he said, sucking the life out of a Dunhill. "But Lycra will only stretch so far."

I KNEW KAREN back when her name wasn't plastered on billboards and buses and full-page newspaper ads and sneakers and baseball caps and perfume bottles and underwear. Back when her name was still Karen Lipsky and she was indeed a size four. But I have to say, I liked her better now that she was heavy. What Karen had gained and never lost after her pregnancy made her more human, more vulnerable than she'd been when I first met her.

I wish I could say it was her incredible talent that had attracted me to go and work for her—her exquisite taste, her ability to design clothes that were sleek and sophisticated and understated, and her legendary loyalty to those who worked for her (not to mention the free and steeply discounted clothes you got if you worked there). But it wasn't really. I hated my job at the time I met her (then as now; some things never change), and the marketing position she was offering me sounded like I might just hate it a little less.

Right after college (University of Michigan), I moved to New York and got a job in advertising (Young & Rubicam) and then another job in advertising (J. Walter Thompson). I was a copy writer at the latter when Karen hired us to position her new company in the market. She had just gone out on her own, having worked her way up, and through, more than a few design houses in the city in the 1970s and 1980s—Halston, Perry Ellis, Gloria Vanderbilt—where she had become known for her bald ambition and raw talent. Especially during the last five years in her position as head in-house designer for Henri Bendel. But though she'd bounced around from house to house, everyone knew where her true inspiration for designing women's fashions had come from: Diane Von Furstenberg. Karen's first job in the business had been as her assistant, and she had never gotten over the wrap dress.

"That dress is genius—pure genius," she'd said in countless interviews and in countless conversations since then. "It was the quintessential 'basic.' The fit, the fabric, the way it hung—I knew the second I put it on that my life was never going to be the same."

And indeed it wasn't. Just before she'd left Bendel's to start her own company, she'd come up with the concept and the design for her own basic: a women's body-suit. Produced in a palette of neutral colors (black, white, brown, navy, gray, for starters), Karen's "second skin" was intended to be the foundation to a woman's wardrobe, over which a suit jacket, pants, sweater, or evening skirt could be worn with ease. Simple and sexy, Karen believed it was to become her signature piece—one that she would take with her when she struck out on her own.

But there was a catch.

The body-suit didn't sell at Bendel's.

And the reason it didn't sell was because another body-suit—exactly the same in design and material—had just hit the market and was flying off the racks in major department stores like Saks and Neiman's and Bloomingdale's, which, unlike Bendel's, had branches all over the country. The success of that designer—Donna Karan—and the untimely coincidence of their both coming out with the same item had haunted Karen ever since. Even after Karen's own star had risen and her success rivaled Donna's, the press always asked her about it. And though they never accused her of copying Donna and though it was clear to them that Karen was immensely talented—more so, the sharpest ones knew, than Donna—that early wrinkle in her career was a scar that in Karen's mind would never ever completely disappear.

But that day seven years ago, during one of the many long strategy meetings Karen insisted on attending at our offices to discuss her new company, I came up, out of sheer desperation, with the idea that she should change her name.

"Change my name?" she said, her skeletal frame turning in her swivel chair to face me. She bit her big lip-sticked lips and stared at me over the plume of smoke coming out of her nose. "What do you mean, *change my name?*"

I had no idea what I meant.

What I *did* know was that she needed to have a corporate identity ready before the fall buying season began, and all we had so far was *LipskyLook*. With that, we'd be lucky if J.C. Penney took her line.

"Maybe the name of your company should relate more to your design philosophy," I heard myself pontificate. "Maybe the name will help connect the wearer to the clothes."

She was still biting her lips, but she hadn't yelled at me yet. Which I took as an encouraging sign.

"A name," I said slowly, gathering all of my bullshitting skills in one glorious breath—I was a copy writer, after all, with layers and layers of creative talent that were, as yet, untapped!—"that describes the woman who will wear your clothes. A name that evokes style. Urbanity. Sophistication. Sex." I came up for air and to buy myself another crucial few seconds of time, and when I did, I noticed her mouth—licked clean of her signature mud-matte pigment and raven-ous for success.

"Lipps," I said suddenly.

Then I wrote it on my pad and held it up so she could see the crucial addition of the second *p*.

"Karen Lipps."

BUT BACK TO that Labor Day weekend, when I started sleeping with the Pickle's Big Bird.

It was a crisp early September Sunday morning, the kind of autumn morning that makes living in downtown New York seem movie-worthy: wisps of white clouds against a bright, clear, relentlessly blue sky; sleek sunglassed people dressed in black jeans and T-shirts on their way into the church of Dean & DeLuca or emerging from the ever-hip NewsBar, holding white paper bags filled with black currant scones or lemon coffee cake or corn-carrot muffins. I myself was walking up University Place with my Starbucks coffee when I noticed a woman—tall and thin with long perfect legs coming out of khaki shorts—pushing a baby stroller toward me. When the light at the corner of Twelfth Street changed and she wheeled the stroller into the crosswalk and revealed the shit-eating grin of a blissfully happy mother, I knew immediately that I had seen that smile before. I just couldn't remember where.

And then it came to me.

High school.

AT SEVENTEEN, AMY Jacobs had been everything I was not. And now, given the child in the stroller, at thirty-five she was obviously still everything I was not.

Back then, she got straight A's and was one of the most attractive girls in the school.

I got straight A's (except for math) and had one eyebrow that grew together.

She was on the varsity field hockey team. And swim team. And gymnastics team.

I was editor in chief of the literary magazine but was short several hundred thousand gym credits by senior year, which almost prevented me from graduating.

She was popular with preppy girls and jocks.

I was popular with the tough girls who kept trying to drag me into the bathroom and dunk my head in the toilet while flushing to give me a "swirlie."

She was dating the cutest nicest smartest boy in the school—well-adjusted adolescent poster-child Jonathan Glebe, a Robby Benson look-alike—advanced placement math, chemistry, French, and English; captain of the soccer team; managing editor of the school newspaper—whom she had been dating since ninth grade. At the end of senior year, they were both headed off to Princeton. And then, of course, they would get married and live happily ever after.

I was not.

I did not.

And so far I had not.

As you can see, I'd really made a lot of progress since the insecurity of my teens.

I froze at the intersection without crossing. I hated moments like this: *to say hello or not to say hello.* Finally something—perhaps the baby—perhaps the fact that I knew, given my state of mind that particular day, that I couldn't take another person asking me if I had a hud-band—tipped the scale of indecision and made me edge a little farther away to make my escape.

But that was not to be.

"Ellen?"

I froze again.

"Ellen Franck?"

I feigned surprise, as if I hadn't been caught trying to hurl myself into oncoming traffic in order to avoid her. "Amy . . . ?" I started. "Amy . . ."

"Jacobs."

"Amy Jacobs." I nodded hazily. "Of course."

"Brookline High School."

"Of *course*."

"Seventeen years," she said, parking the stroller out of the line of foot traffic on the sidewalk and pushing down the wheel brakes. "You look great. And you still have great hair." She rolled her eyes to call my attention to her short straight brown hair. "I always envied your hair."

Amy Jacobs used to envy my hair?

I was shocked.

Still, out of habit, I couldn't resist pulling it out from the sides of my head like Bozo.

"But *you* were the one with the perfect hair." I let the hair drop and then tried, unsuccessfully, to comb my fingers through it. "*You* were the one with *wings*!"

I said *you* as if I were accusing her of something heinous. Which I was: a happy adolescence.

She rolled her eyes again. "Yours is thick. Mine's too thin. Not to mention the bald spot."

I stared at her as she pointed to the front of her head, just above and to the right of her forehead.

"Bald," she said, giggling. "Bald, bald, *bald*."

I almost liked her right then and there.

Who would have believed!

Amy Jacobs going bald and making fun of herself!

But then I remembered.

Jonathan Glebe. Who, I'd heard from someone as miserable during high school as I was, had gone to medical school and become an ob/gyn. An oppressive weight settled over me like a thick dense wet mist when I imagined their perfect life together: his Park Avenue practice; the pregnant women coming and going all day long; their huge fabulous apartment in a nearby doorman building, complete with F.A.O. Schwarz–equipped nursery; her weekly pedicures and manicures; the live-in nanny who was obviously off on Sundays.

It was time to cut this conversation short.

But. I couldn't take my eyes off the Pickle-esque bundle of cuteness in the carriage.

"Great baby," I said, beginning to salivate over the big brown eyes and the pink fleece Baby Gap cardigan and flowered stretchy leggings she had on. Her ensemble reminded me of a similar outfit Nicole had worn at that age. I bent down to touch her silky-smooth blond hair, but ended up kissing her head instead. At such close range her baby-smell made my eyes almost water. I could have eaten her whole.

"Thanks."

"What's her name?"

"Isabel."

"That's a beautiful name. How old is she?"

"Eight months."

Eight months. *Walking?* Maybe. *Talking?* Probably not. *Toilet trained?* Definitely not.

I wasn't really sure. My sister and the Pickle living in New England made it impossible for me to acquire the knowledge of a child's day-to-day minutiae firsthand.

"You must be thrilled," I finally managed.

"We are."

We.

"Do you . . . ?"

"Stay home with her full time? No. We have a nanny."

"A nanny? Sure. That's great."

Dr. Glebe's baby business must be booming.

"Well, I mean, she's full time, but she doesn't live in," she clarified.

I nodded, then felt my stomach drop when I realized the

baby was smiling at me. I bent over and made a big face—
eyes wide open, mouth and tongue making goofy sounds—
then rubbed her stomach until she giggled. See? It wasn't
just Nicole who liked me.

Amy cleared her throat. "So do you—?"

"Have one?" Not unless you counted the Pickle. Oh,
what the hell. "No, but I really want one."

"I know," she said, nodding. I couldn't tell if the expression
on her face was pity or self-satisfied smugness, but whatever
it was, I suddenly wanted to get away from it—and her.

"Well, listen," I said, reining in the initial warmth I'd stu-
pidly let fly because of her female-pattern baldness, "I've got
to run." Then I mumbled something—*big job, big week, big big
big life*—and put my KLNY sunglasses back on.

"Speaking of which, what do you do?" Amy asked. Isabel
had now put all her fingers in her mouth and was smiling—
and drooling—profusely. Adorable.

"I work for Karen Lipps. Marketing director."

So what if I was running out of eggs? At least I had a job.
And *hair*.

"That's great," she said.

"Why? What do you do?"

"I'm a real estate attorney."

"You're a lawyer?"

"What, you hate lawyers?"

"No. It's just that . . . well, I just thought that—you know,
what with a baby and all, you probably wouldn't—"

She waited for me to finish my sentence, but I didn't.

At least not audibly.

*Since you were lucky enough to have a baby, I didn't think you
would also be lucky enough to have a big job.*

Amy suddenly looked uncomfortable, as if she, too, had
had enough of this conversation, confirming my belief that
high school is a place that should never, ever be revisited.

"She's not mine." She blushed, then laughed guiltily. "She's my brother's. Sometimes I just pretend she's mine. I mean, why is that so wrong?" She looked around and grinned without a trace of guilt. "It's not like I do it with people I know. I just do it here. In the park. With strangers. And I don't even do it on purpose. Things just come out of my mouth, and somehow at the time they seem—"

I couldn't believe what I was hearing.

"True," I said. "I know. I do the same thing with my niece. So whatever happened to that boyfriend of yours?"

"Jonathan? It's a long story. What about you? Any potential—"

"Sperm donors? No. Not really. It's a long story, too."

"I'd like to hear it."

"Well, we should get together sometime," I said. "Form our own Imaginary Mommy Group."

"I could get a sitter."

"Or we could just double up on your nanny."

She laughed and reached into her bag to get out her date book. "This is a bad week, though."

"For me too," I said, flipping through my ten-pound multilayered multitiered multitabbed color-coded-insert date book. "And the next two weeks aren't much better: I've got two weddings and a baby shower."

"I've got two baby showers and a briss."

Then, after going through about twenty-three possible lunch-drinks-dinner dates, we finally settled on one—dinner, on a Thursday, three weeks hence.

"By the way," I said, "do you like your job?"

"No. Do you?"

"No."

We smiled, then exchanged business cards.

I had a feeling we were finally going to become close friends.

4

. . .

NOT THAT I needed any more friends, really.

I had quite enough already.

Or so I thought.

And yet in retrospect I see that the ones who were single or childless had been dwindling steadily for years without my really noticing.

First there were the recent couplings:

Lisa: *Engaged.*

Katie: *Engaged.*

Nicky: *Engaged.*

Then there were the semirecent betrothals:

Susan: *Married six months.*

Jill: *Married one year.*

Cathy: *Married two years.*

And then there were the ones who had been quietly building families for a while now:

Julia: *Married six years. Two children: five and two.*

Anne: *Divorced twice. One five-year-old.*

Rachel: *Not married. No boyfriend. Sperm bank baby on the way.*

And of course, my sister:
Married five years.
One Pickle.

I had only three close female friends left who were single and childless—Francine, a friend from Michigan who was now a high-school English teacher in Los Angeles; Jana, a fellow copy writer from Young & Rubicam I'd bonded with my first day there; and Renee, my best friend at work—four now, if you counted Amy. So since she was the only one who wanted children, her appearance, or reappearance, was rather fortuitous, not to mention comforting, given the eerie similarity of our Familial Infant Envy Disorder pathologies.

IN THE WEEKS between the time Amy and I had run into each other, I found myself worrying about our upcoming dinner—not because I was nervous but because I was afraid of disappointment. I'd felt such a spark, such a rush of instant camaraderie when we'd started talking—a kindred spirit, someone who understood that the raging lunacy of Familial Infant Envy Disorder wasn't really raging lunacy at all but merely the visible manifestation of our normal natural biological urges to procreate and to connect with someone outside of ourselves. While my other friends—those with children and without—and even my sister—accepted this part of my personality and didn't attempt to talk me out of it (wanting to mother was a positive urge, after all, unlike, say, wanting to snort heroin), I never mistook their acceptance for true understanding. Until Amy—until that moment on the sidewalk when she tried to lie about her niece being her daughter and we both came clean, finishing each other's sentences in the process—I'd always felt more than a little bit crazy.

In the three weeks before our dinner date, I tried to convince myself that people did change—especially after seventeen years. After all, it wasn't like Amy had been carrying her field hockey stick or wearing her varsity letter jacket when we'd met—though in my elephants-never-forget geekdom-is-forever mind, she might as well have. The assumptions I'd made, the snap judgments based on that brief vision of her on the sidewalk in front of me—*she was married with a child, and therefore happy, and therefore also winning*—were nothing if not proof of the fact that it was me who hadn't changed. That despite the passage of time and all the "personal growth" that supposedly went with it—the career achievements; the years of therapy with their requisite epiphanies and behavior-altering breakthroughs; the romantic relationships that hopefully become less and less pathological the older and wiser you become—I was, deep down, insecure and mistrustful of people who seemed to have it too easy in life. Like Amy. Whether her life had been sheer misery from graduation day until now or had been movie perfect shouldn't have mattered to me for the reasons it did. Her success did not ipso facto mean my failure, or vice versa. And before I saw her again, I had to get over the years when in my mind it did.

I HAD MADE a seven-thirty reservation for us at Café Loup, a softly lit, deeply pretentious French bistro on West Thirteenth Street. Even though she lived on the Upper West Side, Amy said she didn't mind meeting all the way downtown—we were both coming from midtown right after work anyway—and I was glad she'd agreed. The older I'd gotten, the more intolerant I'd become of noisy restaurants where you couldn't hear what the person sitting across from you was saying. Among other things.

"Wait!" I said when we first sat down, interrupting a

hilarious anecdote Amy was telling about a recent diaper change that went awry on someone's Oriental rug. "I want to know what you've been doing since 1980."

"You mean, we should put this mental illness in context," she said.

"Exactly."

I liked this woman. Even though she probably wasn't perverse enough to have a copy of the *Diagnostic and Statistical Manual* (the bible of all shrinks) sitting on her coffee table as I did, she understood what we were dealing with here.

"Do I have to go all the way back to high school?"

"No," I said magnanimously, as if I were about to let her off the hook. "Just go back to after high school."

"Which is when it all started to go downhill."

She took a sip from her glass of wine and then took a deep breath as if she were summoning up the energy needed to tell seventeen years' worth of personal history in one sentence.

"Okay. You remember Jonathan. Well, after high school, we went to Princeton together. I was an English major, and he was pre-med. And all along it was . . . well, it was assumed that we were going to get married. We talked about marriage. His parents talked about marriage. My parents talked about marriage. It was just a question of when. Obviously we were going to wait—definitely until he was in medical school and probably until after he graduated." She picked up her glass of wine and let it rest against her cheek.

"So we graduated," she continued. "He and I both got into Columbia—me for law school—I was going to change the world like Mr. Collacci"—our American history teacher—"told us to. Not that becoming a real estate lawyer is a world-changing profession. But anyway we moved here. We studied. We graduated. We stayed so he could do his internship and residency here. I got an associate's position at

Davis, Polk, and we found a great co-op on West Seventy-second Street, which his parents paid for: an early engagement gift."

"And this was, what," I asked, doing a quick mental calculation, "seven years ago?" I was trying to remember what I was doing then: closing on my own co-op; recovering from a particularly nasty breakup with Ross, a coworker at J. Walter Thompson; giving notice at J. Walter Thompson in the wake of that breakup—but not because of it—and going to work for Karen Lipps, Inc., full time.

"Seven."

"Sorry. Go on."

"And then we got engaged. And then we started planning the wedding—which is when I started to wonder what I was getting myself into."

The waiter arrived, clearing away our salads and returning with our steaks—hers rare and mine well done. We were both PMS and ravenous, as it turned out, and were momentarily distracted by all that meat.

"Why did you start to wonder then? I mean, you'd been together since eleventh grade or something."

"Ninth grade, actually," she said, trying to suppress an uncontrollable laugh.

I still couldn't believe that people had boyfriends in ninth grade. Or in twelfth grade, for that matter. But since I wanted to hear the rest of her story, I let it drop. "So you suddenly realized . . ."

"Something had been missing for a long time, and I suddenly realized I couldn't ignore it anymore."

"What was missing?"

She shrugged, then looked a little sheepish. "In a nutshell?"

I nodded.

"Sex."

I could relate to that. The absence of it, that is.

"We never did it anymore. I mean, maybe once in a while, after I chased him around the bed, which would make me feel completely pathetic."

I put my knife and fork down. No one would believe this either: Amy Jacobs chasing Jonathan Glebe around the bed for sex.

"Did you ever talk about it?"

"I tried to, but he never seemed to think anything was wrong with our relationship. He didn't seem to think that never having sex with the person you were with was abnormal."

Wait till she heard my story.

"So it wasn't that he didn't want to get married."

"No. In fact, he was incredibly enthusiastic about it. I mean, of the two of us, he was definitely much more engaged in the details and mechanics of it. What the date was going to be. Where it was going to be. How many people there would be. What the food would be. Please. He could have told Martha Stewart a thing or two.

"So then about two months before the wedding—the invitations had been printed but not sent yet—I finally found out what the problem was. He was gay."

I blinked wildly.

"How did you find out?"

"Jonathan told me." She smiled and pushed her plate away. "One night after chasing him around the bed—and getting nowhere—I called him a faggot." She looked embarrassed suddenly, as much by her use of the word as what had provoked her to use it. "And he sat down on the bed and said, 'Yes, I am a faggot.' And that was it. Twelve years over, just like that. I moved out two days later. Back to my parents' house on Long Island. Where I stayed for six months until I could face starting all over again."

I'd heard about women actually marrying men they didn't know were gay, but I had never personally known anyone who had had such a close call. How you would ever again trust your judgment about people, how you would ever trust your perceptions enough to think that you were probably right, or at least not completely, incredibly, out-in-left-field wrong—not to mention how you got to the point where you could tell your story with a modicum of dignity the way Amy just had—seemed to me to be an amazing achievement. But . . . how long had he known? Had he been planning on telling her? If so, when had he planned on telling her? After the waiter cleared our plates, I asked her.

"I don't know. He wouldn't really say. But I think he'd known for a long time, probably since high school. Which makes the whole relationship even more of a farce than it already was." We each leaned away as the waiter brought us our coffee. "Needless to say," she continued, "I canceled the wedding and returned the ring. But I still have the dress. You know, in the unlikely event that somebody ever asks me to marry them again."

I wondered how she could have been with Jonathan for so long and not known this crucial element of his being, of his personality, but maybe it wasn't that hard to believe. Hadn't I been involved with someone for about a year before finding out that he had a twin brother? Hadn't I not known twice, with two different men, that I was being cheated on? When you're young and naive and you want something or someone badly enough—in Amy's case, marriage and a doctor-husband and a normal life; in my case, connection, regardless of the duration—you can somehow manage not to see the big huge pink elephants in the room.

"And then?"

"And then my mother died." She lowered her eyes.

"I'm sorry."

"Thanks. We were really close." She managed a slight smile before going on. "So now, two years after my mother and five years after Jonathan and after the longest dating dryspell in history, I'm seeing Will. Who's either just about to finish his dissertation and get his Ph.D. in American literature from NYU or on the brink of complete failure and financial ruin."

"How old is he?"

"Thirty-eight."

"Cute?"

"Very."

"Sexual orientation?"

"Straight."

"You're sure?"

"Positive."

"Sex?"

"He can't get enough of me."

"Are you in love?"

"Completely."

I knew there had to be something wrong with this picture, since there was something wrong with every picture.

"So . . . the problem is . . . ?"

"The problem is, he's not ready for living together. Or marriage. Or even *discussing* living together. Or marriage. Which is why I'm so niece obsessed. Because at this rate, discussing children will probably have to wait until well into the new millennium."

Which was a big problem since Amy's gum-ball machine was also running low on eggs.

"So," she said, as we both stirred our cups of decaf and attacked a finger-thick slice of flourless chocolate cake, "no humiliating engagement to someone who turned out to be gay?"

No, I told her. Just the semiserious college boyfriend whom I loved in that unformed, incomplete, clueless way you do when you're too young to know any better.

And the line of short-lived boyfriends who'd fallen away like toy soldiers during the years when I still felt I was young and had my whole life ahead of me.

Then the one who broke my heart badly and without warning.

Then the one I would have wanted to marry if he hadn't already been married.

And then the point at which I started to feel as if I'd crossed over from being an eligible young unmarried woman to one of those women who had never gotten married.

"So now," I said, picking up at the present, "I'm in an ex*tremely* promising relationship." I laughed here to affect maximum irony.

"With?"

"Malcolm."

"Who is . . . ?"

"Forty-seven."

"Attractive?"

"Very."

"How long have you been seeing him?"

"About six months."

"Ever married?"

"Once. Divorced."

"Children?"

"Had one. A son." I took a deep breath. "Who died, five years ago."

She winced, then whispered, "How?"

"Leukemia."

"Jesus."

"I know. He'd just turned seven."

She looked at me to get a sense of what to say next, and when I shook my head and shrugged, she went on. "Job?"

"Writer."

She raised an eyebrow. "What's his name?"

"South. M. C. South."

"Sure. I've heard of him. He's famous."

Was famous.

"He wrote about inner-city schools, didn't he?"

"For *The New York Times.* Which won a Pulitzer."

She nodded, duly impressed. "But he's written books, too, hasn't he?"

"Two. But he hasn't published any in a while." In over a decade. "He wrote for magazines for a long time after that," I continued. "*Esquire. New York* magazine. *The New Yorker.* Now he teaches at The New School. That's how we met. I took a class he teaches there." I thought of the CV he'd handed out that first night along with the syllabus; how intrigued I was by it. "He says he's a has-been. But I like to think he's at the end of a severe downward trajectory and poised for a comeback."

"So," she said, officially opening up the topic of Malcolm for discussion.

"So. The problems. One: He's depressed, due to the fact that his career isn't what it used to be, after what's happened in his personal life over the last decade or so. Two: He's taking Prozac, so he's not really, you know . . ."

"Interested in sex?"

I tilted my head and raised an eyebrow. How did she know that?

"Will was on it for a few months last year after he missed another big deadline. But then he realized that because of that particular side effect, he was better off *off* the medication."

"Unfortunately, I don't think the same would be true for Malcolm."

"Doesn't sound like it."

"And three," I continued, and here was the clinker: "While he's brilliant and funny and weird and interesting and confused about everything, of one thing he is absolutely certain: He does not want any more children, given what happened to the last one."

"I don't even know where to begin," she said finally.

And neither did I, really.

I ran my hands through my hair and tried to get a handle on how to explain him and our relationship—not just for Amy's sake but for my own as well: Whenever I tried to deconstruct the complicated elements of our situation and examine the sum of its parts, it always left me confused and a little sad, as if I'd lost something I wasn't sure I'd ever really had.

"This is going to sound crazy," I said, "but despite the downside—the rather obvious, inescapable, problematic, and deeply ironic downside—we're really good together, I think. We eat together. Sleep together. Spend weekends together. And since we don't have sex, we talk all the time. So I mean, except for feeling like I'm dating Big Bird—a big, large, funny, weird, kind, strange, generous, sexless sort-of-boyfriend—"

"Who's walking down Sesame Street schlepping an awful lot of baggage—" she added.

"I've actually never been in such a normal relationship."

"Or been so well rested."

"Or well fed."

Or unafraid.

5

. . .

MALCOLM HADN'T ALWAYS been frozen—just since he met me.

Or so he says.

Which is not as bad as it sounds, since he met me right about the time he started taking the libido-deadening antidepressants and also around the time that his career took one last big nosedive plunge into has-been obscurity. But I suspect his intimacy problems began long before me, sometime after his son died and sometime after his marriage collapsed under the weight of all that grief.

Which led to his drinking.

Which led to his profound writer's block.

Which, as it turned out, led to me, when I took his night course at The New School on the history of print journalism last winter semester.

And so we met.

Ours was, by anyone's standards, including my own, an unremarkable beginning: a question I asked one cold, cold night after the second class, which he answered; then a self-deprecating remark I made about my job, to which he responded more directly than I'd expected.

"So why do you do it?" he asked.

"Because I don't know what else to do."

He smiled ironically, and when he did, it made me feel as if he'd chosen me to share in some secret private joke. "I can understand that. And why else?"

It was mid-February; bleak. I looked out the third-floor classroom window past our glassy reflections into the cold blackness beyond. "Because I can't do anything else."

"I can understand that, too. Only in your case, it's clearly not true."

"Why in my case?"

"Because in your case, as opposed to mine, you're young."

"I'm thirty-five. That's not so young."

"Oh, yes it is. When you're staring down the barrel at fifty, it's very, very young." He rubbed his face where his beard would have been if he'd had one—a face that, at most, could easily have passed for forty-two or forty-three—the skin lined only between the brows and around the mouth; his eyes deep brown surrounded by clear whites; his thick straight hair still dark, with only a few strands of gray here and there. "And obviously you're quite capable, otherwise you wouldn't have the job that you have—distasteful and repulsive as you've just told me you think it is."

I looked at him sitting on the edge of the desk with his arms crossed in front of him. He was tall and broad-shoul-dered, and with his sleeves rolled up and his tie loosened, I could almost imagine what he would have looked like, been like, fifteen years ago at the peak of his career—command-ing, consumed, impassioned.

"You'll figure it out," he said. "When you're ready. You'll quit this thing and find something else to do."

"How do you know that?" I asked, though what I really

wanted to know was how he could see my future when I
couldn't see it myself.

"Because." He turned and started collecting the notes and
books he'd spread out on the desk at the beginning of his
lecture. "Because I suspect you do know what you want to
do next, but you're not ready."

I felt myself blush, not only from having been found out
but from the secret thrill, the flattery, of being read, of being
seen so clearly.

"Maybe," I lied.

He turned back to me and hooked my eyes, daring me to tell
him what it was. But I didn't. I didn't know him well enough to
admit that what I wanted to do next was have a Pickle.

"ANY GUY *THAT* old who *isn't* married is either a wacko or a
fag," Renee declared when I told her about the previous
night's rare verbal exchange with a man.

It was seven-thirty—early for our office and early for me,
since I usually came in around ten—and that was on good
days—but not early for her. Renee was always in by seven,
and her work ethic and obsessive need to be organized at the
beginning of every day was only part of her arrival time. She
had the kind of insomnia where you wake up in the middle
of the night—four A.M., you could set your watch to it, she
always said—so after the early morning back-to-back
episodes of *Perry Mason,* she'd go to the gym and then head
to work, where, once she'd straightened up her already-
straightened office and desk, she'd make a list of things she
needed to do that day. Seven cups of coffee and ten cigarettes
later, I'd arrive and she'd torture me. And then she'd really
wake up.

Coming in so early, I'd thrown her off. She took an extra-
long drag from one of her Marlboros and raised her eyebrows

when I walked into her office, explaining that the reason I'd gotten to work way before I normally did was because I hadn't fallen asleep. I sat down in one of her twin pea-green wool-upholstered armchairs and drank my take-out latte.

"These things are so"—I looked at the white sip-lid on my paper coffee cup—"infantile. I mean, look at this—this gigantic plastic—"

"Nipple," Renee finished.

"Exactly. People walking up and down the street, in offices, airports, sucking, sucking, sucking. It's unseemly."

She looked completely uninterested. "So?"

"So what?"

"So which is he?"

I shook my head dismissively, the way I always did whenever she made some ridiculously overreaching generalization that I suspected, deep down, was completely true. At forty-five, Renee Friedman was the head designer of our new menswear line—still in production but getting ready to debut in the fall—and my closest friend at work. She was as cynical and jaded as it was possible to become without killing yourself or having someone else kill you—a personality flaw she continually blamed on "a lifetime of dating wackos and designing for fags"—and yet few people besides me knew that she would have given both legs and an arm for a man who loved her.

Wacko or fag?

Wacko or fag?

How was I supposed to know?

"Well, how was he dressed?" she asked, lighting another cigarette and blowing the smoke into my face for emphasis.

"Like a guy. A regular guy," I said—*guy* being a kind of code word for *not gay*. "A suit," though the jacket had hung on the back of his chair the whole class and not been worn. "White shirt. Armani tie."

"Too bad it wasn't Versace. Then it would have been a dead giveaway, since only pimps and fags wear Versace." She paused to inspect a possible lintball on her black cashmere V-neck sweater that was tucked into gray wool men's trousers. "So conservative, basically. Not self-conscious. No pleated pants. No Prada briefcase. No Gucci loafers."

No. No. And no.

Yet she remained as unconvinced as always. To Renee, all men were fags until proven otherwise. "Then he's a wacko."

I shook my head again. "I don't think so."

"You don't *think* so. That's definitive."

"Look, he was a really famous writer once. And now he's teaching."

"At the Learning Annex."

"No. At The New School."

"Whatever."

"There is a difference, you know."

She shrugged. "So why don't you just ask him?"

"Ask him what?"

"Ask him which he is. Just go up to him after the next class and say, 'Excuse me, Mr. Whatever-Your-Name-Is: Given the fact that you're *so* old and *not* married, are you a wacko or a fag?' That's what I would do."

"You would not."

"I would, too."

"Bullshit."

"Fuck you. Fine. Don't ask him," she said, clearly disgusted with me and turning to her to-do list instead. "Just don't come whining to me when you find out he's one or the other. Or both."

I WOULD HAVE no way of finding out anything about Malcolm for the next two weeks. Karen had forced me to attend a big AIDS-benefit silent-auction industry dinner she was cohosting with her nemesis Donna Karan on the following Thursday night—class night.

"I need all my friends around me," she'd said with what could almost be called humility—rare for her. "You know how Donna hates me." So I grudgingly attended, though I spent most of the evening ignoring the speeches and thinking about Malcolm.

Through the Internet, I had already searched for the books he'd written—*Broken Promises,* which he'd expanded from his *New York Times* series on education, and *The Bankrupting of Manhattan*—and had ordered them both in paperback. I had also done a Nexus search at the office and printed out a stack of material about him—reviews of his books; features written about him when he'd won the Pulitzer; articles he'd written over the years for magazines. Though inspired by innocent curiosity, my information-gathering made me feel as if I'd spent the week moonlighting as a private investigator, and when I walked toward his desk after his lecture, I couldn't help feeling a little guilty.

"Where were you last week?" he asked after class.

When I told him, he smiled slyly. "I thought maybe after our conversation, you decided to go off and do the thing you wouldn't tell me you want to do."

"I'm afraid I'm not that impulsive."

"That surprises me."

"Why?"

"I don't know." He shrugged as if he'd revealed too much by letting me know he'd given me, and what I'd said the previous week, some thought. "I guess you strike me as being strong-willed. Someone who might, one day, out of the blue, walk away from something and never come back."

Or walk away from some*one* and never come back, I later realized he must have meant, too.

"Who, me?" I said, making a big face. "I'm the exact opposite of that. I'm a clinger. I hate change. I'm always the last one to leave a job. Always the last one to leave a relationship. Always the last one to—"

"Leave class?" he said, leading me out the door. "Want to get a drink?"

IT WAS UNSEASONABLY warm for a night in early March as Malcolm and I walked east across Twelfth Street and then down University Place to the Cedar Tavern, a dark old bar where all the great painters in the 1950s drank—Jackson Pollock, Willem de Kooning, Jasper Johns. Now, though, it was just a slightly run-down, slightly seedy fallback place in the neighborhood when you couldn't think of anywhere else to go. There were two empty seats at the bar, and he led me toward them, pulling my stool out slightly as I dropped my bags to the floor.

He ordered a Coke with lemon, and I ordered a mineral water with ice and lime, and when our drinks, or "soft drinks" as Malcolm referred to them, arrived, we got very busy with our straws and wedges of fruit, stirring and squeezing and stirring again.

"In case you haven't guessed, I don't drink anymore," Malcolm said. "I thought I'd just mention it now in the spirit of full disclosure."

"I guessed." I didn't drink much myself anymore. Somewhere along the line, alcohol had stopped making me feel young and happy and had started leaving me feeling very old and very tired.

"You're observant," he said with more than a hint of sarcasm. "What gave me away?"

"Oh, I don't know." I turned to face him, close enough now to look straight into his eyes and see the resignation in them. "Because most writers drink," I finally said. "Especially journalists." I didn't want to say that his face had that slightly ravaged look of someone who'd been farther down the sort of road in life I always feared I'd end up on myself—the kind filled with pain and loss and solitude and grief. "It was just a lucky guess," I added quickly.

He sucked an ice cube into his mouth and chewed it.

"You're kind," he said. "Maybe too kind."

"You can never be too kind. Kindness is a rare commodity these days."

"I'd agree with that. But it was kind of you anyway to refer to me as a writer when I'm really not one anymore."

"Yes, you are."

He sucked in another ice cube. "I'm a teacher."

"You're a writer *and* a teacher."

He let the statement drop unrebutted, and we talked then for a while about other things.

About the class.

About the books he'd written.

About the city and how we each felt about living in it.

About a lot of things that were easy to slip in and out of.

And as we did, I sensed that whatever it was that had derailed him had left him lost; stranded; unable to feel his way back to where he'd been before.

"You miss it, writing," I said quietly, more a statement than a question.

He seemed momentarily distracted by the muted basketball game on the television set above the bar.

"I do," he said finally. "But not as much as I miss other things."

"What other things?"

He finished his drink, then started to reach into his pocket for his wallet to settle the bill.

"That's a very long story, and not one you would want me to tell you tonight."

From the sound of his voice, I could tell the subject was closed for now.

"Trust me," he said, leading me toward the door. "Come on. I'll take you home."

I lived just a few blocks from the Cedar Tavern, and except for the sound of our shoes on the pavement, we walked together in silence most of the way. It was still early—just after ten—and unusually quiet for a weeknight in the Village. While we'd been in the bar, it had rained, and the streets, still wet and shiny slick, caused the tires of taxis going by to make a soft sticky sound. Malcolm walked me up to my brownstone—my home, my refuge, for the last six years, the longest I'd lived any-where since leaving my parents' house.

He stopped, then stood there awkwardly, his hands deep in his pockets.

"Thanks," he said finally.

"For what?"

"For the conversation."

"You don't have to thank me for that. I enjoyed it."

"I enjoyed it, too."

A few more seconds passed in silence before I asked him if he wanted to come in.

"I don't have any Coke, but I have about ten different kinds of water."

"Another time," he said, his voice barely above a whisper.

"Oh. Well. Okay." I instinctively stepped back, embar-rassed that he might have found my invitation too aggressive, or simply one that he was not interested in accepting.

"I'll see you, Ellen" was all he said before he turned and walked away toward the distant lights of Sixth Avenue.

THE ONLY EXPLANATION I have for getting involved with someone who was frozen was that I didn't know he was frozen at the time. And when I did find out, it was too late—too late to change directions; too late to pull myself away from someone who seemed to need so much. Who seemed to need *me* so much. And who I would come to need, too.

Even the first night he came into my apartment and stayed over after a month of postclass Cedar Tavern conversations, I didn't know. That first night we spent together, I chalked it up to the conversation we'd had earlier in the evening, when he'd told me, finally, about his son; his wife; his family; his career—about everything he'd lost. This was the kind of conversation you can't quite walk away from when it's over, and so when we stood in front of my apartment and I touched his arm and he didn't move away, I took it as a signal. I tugged at the shirt cuff at his wrist, then slipped my hand into his and led him up the steps, through the set of double doors in the foyer, then up the flight of stairs to my apartment.

Once inside, he stood in the center of the living room while I dropped my bags and went to turn on a small lamp by the bookshelf in the corner. I knew his mind was working, taking in as many details as possible. To anyone who didn't know what he'd done for a living for so long and with such skill, he might have seemed as if he were simply trying to get his bearings in unfamiliar territory. But as I moved around the room and into the kitchen to get our water, I watched his eyes dart from point to point. From books, to small framed photographs of Lynn and Paul and Nicole on the shelves, to papers on the desk, to my bedroom door beyond, I knew that he was assessing me, deconstructing me, trying to understand me.

I sat down on the couch and put our water glasses on the table in front of me.

"What are you thinking?" I asked.

He looked at me out of the corner of his eye and pretended to be preoccupied only with the range and scope of books on my shelves.

"I was just thinking that you must read a lot."

"I used to. But I don't anymore," I said, responding to his statement but knowing he was really thinking about whether he should leave my apartment before anything happened.

I tried to read him—tried to decide if I should say something then about how we didn't have to sleep together tonight if he didn't want to, or that we could if he did want to—that it didn't matter—that after the conversation we'd had, all I wanted was to be with him. But before I knew which way to go, he walked slowly over to the couch and sat down. He looked down at my hands, which were gripping my knees, and then he leaned closer and touched the side of my face.

And then he kissed me.

It was an unusual kiss, I remember thinking at the time: awkward but passionate; tentative yet urgent in the sense that he seemed to be willing himself over a cliff—as though kissing a woman were an experience he had long since imagined and anticipated yet greatly feared. I remember noticing that he was shaking—his whole body—but I remember feeling certain the shaking would disappear as soon as the lights were off, as soon as we were in bed and our bodies had had a chance to get used to each other; the way that shyness and awkwardness always did the first time.

I stood up, and he followed me down the short hallway to my bedroom. As we stood next to the bed, he put his hands on my hips to turn me toward him, then he put his hands on either side of my face and bent to kiss me again. He slid his hands over my throat and slowly down my neck to the cardigan sweater that started there, and when his fingers found the small white buttons, he undid them, one by one, sliding the sweater off my shoulders and onto the floor. It was dark, very dark in my room, and before I closed my eyes, I felt him lay one hand at the small of my back and the other flat against my chest bone, and then his finger slowly traced a half circle around the front of my neck, as if he were following the line of an invisible necklace. We sat down on the bed and took the rest of our clothes off, and once we had, I was startled by how powerful, how graceful his body was—the thick bands of muscles down his back and down his legs; the incredible smoothness of his skin against mine when he slid into bed next to me.

"I like your perfume," he whispered, and then a few minutes later, "I like being with you." His arms tightened around me, but he didn't touch me further than this embrace.

I put my head on his chest and listened to his heart, and though I was not in love with him yet and didn't know whether I ever could be, that moment of simple human contact made my eyes blur with tears. It had been a long time, a very long time, since someone without a wife to go home to had held me in the dark.

"Would you mind if we didn't do this tonight?" he whispered. "It's been," he continued slowly, "a long time since I've been with a woman, and I don't think I'd be very good at it right now."

"That's okay," I said. And it was.

So we lay there instead, waiting for sleep, my arms around him as far as they could go. As if I could embrace the whole of his injury. And contain it. And heal it.

6

. . .

SUDDENLY IT HAD become apparent that Karen Lipps
was gaining weight.

It was about one month after Fashion Week—a long
month of follow-up calls to key buyers and retailers about
our spring line and making sure that our current couture
pieces were being worn by enough famous people to possibly make the weekly columns—and I was exhausted.

I was also bored. I was no marketing genius. I knew that.
But I did my job, and I did it well. I was competent, detail
oriented, deadline conscious, and I saw and understood the
Big Picture: people. That might not sound like much, but it
was. Marketing was about selling, and selling was about talking, and if there was one thing I could do it was talk.
Especially over lunch.

First there was the gossip.

Gossip.

Gossip.

Gossip.

Then the perfect harmless flattering Karen-anecdote

("Do you know how she got her inspiration for the drape of her long raw silk evening skirt?" Lean in. "She took a Polaroid of the shower curtain in her hotel room last year when she was in Paris for the spring shows!")

Or office anecdote ("No, Simon's not from England! He's from New Jersey!").

Then a little business at the end, about what they'd be stupid not to buy ("If Karen's doing a short jacket again for fall, you know everyone else is going to do a shorter jacket, too." "Ralph's doing flats like ours, only with a square-ish toe again—which is *so* last year. And Calvin? Who knows. Who cares. He's starting to make Enzo Angiolini and Nine West look original").

Which was what Karen needed. Someone she could trust, who knew her when but didn't divulge her secrets. She didn't need someone with something to prove, someone whose ego might eclipse her own. She was the genius. She had the talent. Sure, she'd go to her grave trying to prove to herself and everyone else that she came up with the body-suit idea before Donna Karan. But her clothes were so good, they could have sold themselves (were such a thing possible in this day and age), and everybody knew it.

Sometimes, though, I had trouble with even the basics.

Existential trouble.

Like, not caring.

Sometimes it happened when I was sitting with a buyer, trying to sell him or her on a new pant style ("Fuller, shorter." "Longer, leaner."). Or why their store should give us more floor space or better floor space or reduce another designer's floor space. ("Liz Claiborne is like a virus! Everytime you get off an elevator in a women's department, there it is! Liz! Liz! Liz! Enough with the Liz Claiborne already!") Or on the exquisiteness of a particular fashion— the new lines of a suit or the new cut of a blouse Karen was working on, or the "vision" behind her "artistic decision" to stay with the mock turtleneck for another season instead of returning to the ubiquitous high-scoop T-shirt. ("Quite frankly, Karen's tired of the neck. She believes very strongly that the neck is a very intimate part of the body, almost a private part of the body, and that it should not be so exposed. You could say the Victorian's ankle is Karen's neck—it's so much more alluring if it's hidden and there's the element of surprise.") A little voice would creep into my head—creep behind my eyes and down into the back of my throat and it would whisper this:

They're just clothes.

They're just clothes.

By that October, the voice was creeping into my head more than it ever had before, and I knew my days in the business were numbered.

So that Monday morning I took my time getting to the office—a little too much time, drinking coffee and doing the crossword puzzle in bed. I was about an hour later than usual I realized when I saw the giant clock as I entered the building. As it turned out my arrival was exquisitely timed with Karen's.

I had just stepped onto the elevator in the lobby, and right as the doors were about to shut, I saw a fat dimpled arm reach between the automated door and the metal casing of the elevator. The arm was followed by a huge bosom, and then by the solid bulge of a hip and thigh. Then one fat foot stuffed into a black suede loafer appeared, and then the other, until a large figure dressed all in black stood next to me, breathless.

Only when I saw her pull her black sweater over her leg-ging-ed behind and angle her backside into the far corner of the elevator did I realize it was Karen. I almost hadn't recognized her. She'd been away for the past three weeks in

Europe—trawling for fabrics and inspiration—and she hadn't been due to return until the following week.

The hiding of her behind was something I'd never really noticed in all the time I'd worked for her, until Gail, her sister, had pointed it out to me a few years ago during a visit to the office.

"Have you ever noticed how Karen will never let you see her ass?" Gail had said as the three of us sat in Karen's office. Karen had just managed somehow to get up from her desk, shut her door, then sit down again without once turning her back to us.

She and Karen had the same giant lips and underbites and the same long chins that jutted out farther than they should, but Gail was softer, rounder, less angular. I liked her. She was funny, with none of the hardness or cynicism that was the hallmark of the die-hard New Yorker. Gail had three children and a periodontist husband, and every few weeks she'd come in from Long Island for lunch and shopping and a quick visit with her exciting and famous sibling. Like Lynn, Gail didn't seem to mind that her younger sister had, at least on the surface, a more glamorous life than she did. In fact, they both seemed to enjoy hearing about our work-stress: it made their own intense domestic-stress sound like a walk in the park.

"No, I never noticed."

She turned to me in disbelief.

"What do you mean, you've never noticed? How could you not have noticed? Ever since she and I were kids, she's been backing out of rooms. Walking backward to avoid turning around. Angling herself around corners or up against walls to prevent anyone from seeing it. I don't even think her husband's seen it. Not that her ass needs to be hidden like my ass needs to be hidden."

She stood up and turned so that her back was to me. "*I'm*

the one who should be backing out of rooms." She grabbed
the bags of flesh that were her buttocks so hard, her hands
made a slapping sound against them. *"Look at this!"* she said,
peering around to see my reaction before sitting down.

Karen half-swiveled nervously in her chair and tried to
smile. She took a sip of bottled water from her glass and
popped an Altoids mint into her mouth: *lunch*.

"I don't know what's so wrong with your ass that you
won't let anybody see it," Gail continued.

"It's *wide*," Karen finally said, enunciating through
clenched teeth. "And it's *flat*."

Gail turned to me again. "She's ill," she said. "My sister is
ill. Don't you think she's ill?"

Since that time, I'd been acutely aware of Karen's secret
"part," as I was that morning in the elevator, only this time I
couldn't afford to indulge myself in the hilarity of her neu-
rosis or in my shock at the reason for her hugeness: I had to
say hello. I took my sunglasses off and checked my posture.

"Good *morning*!" I said with exaggerated cheerfulness.
Though Karen knew that I was good at my job and had
grown quite dependent on me in that regard, her one com-
plaint about me had always been what she perceived to be
my negative attitude. Or oddness, as she sometimes called it.
This, she felt, was primarily manifested by my facial expression—furrow-browed, unsmiling, and altogether too serious
for someone in the fashion business. Karen Lipps expected
those who worked for her—her "family," as she always
referred to us without a trace of irony—to be happy.

And, up until she had Marissa, to never have children.

"None of you better ever get pregnant," she used to say to
Renee and Annette and me whenever someone she knew in
the business announced they were going to have a child.
"Because if you do, I'll have to fire you." She'd smile at us
then with her alien blue eyes and her slightly too-long obvi-

ously capped teeth and reach for her bottled water and a breath mint.

And while we were never quite sure whether she meant it or not, we were sure about this: Karen Lipps would never be a mother.

"Which is fine with me since I never want kids, either," Renee would say.

And which was fine with me, too, since it was before my egg-filled gum-ball machine appeared and began to embody my existential angst, and since I'd already decided that Karen should never have children even if she wanted them because she was a Vulcan: Looks human. Acts human. Seems human. *Not* human.

Only Annette, who was from a big Italian family in Queens where having children was like eating and breathing, would look shocked and disgusted and dissolve into silence.

"That woman is *sick,*" she'd say, rushing back to her office as if to escape whatever disease Karen carried and was trying to spread.

Those of us who had been with her since the beginning of her meteoric rise in the fashion business knew Karen's fierce ambition; her ability to play the master chess game of corporate politics; her obsession with her work and her intolerance of anything and anyone that interfered with it. And we had a hard time believing that she'd mellowed in her second marriage and that the birth of her daughter had softened her and made her see, finally, that there were more important things in life besides money and fame and licensing deals. And skeletal thinness.

Yet it was hard to be sure.

Karen's husband, Arthur Klein, a short, quiet, balding man famous for collecting art and channeling his family's vast wealth into philanthropic causes, worked at home and functioned, more or less, as vice-nanny and house-husband—allowing his wife to sustain the same grueling work and social schedule she'd had before the baby. But something had changed. Where once her life had been an open book for self-promotion—homes shot for the architectural/decor glossies; lengthy interviews given for profiles in the women's magazines; beauty rituals, exercise regimes, and spa vacations divulged and documented to anyone with a circulation over two million—now it was not. Karen had closed the curtain on her life and allowed no one—no journalist, no photographer, not even a staff member—to penetrate the new force field of privacy she'd created. The only thing that was unclear was who she was trying to protect behind that veil of silence: her daughter or herself.

It took a few seconds for Karen to acknowledge me in that tiny elevator, and in that short time I noticed the little beads of sweat that had appeared on her upper lip, making me wonder momentarily if she might not be well. She wiped herself quickly with a tissue and then turned to me.

"How was your trip?" I asked.

"Productive. I've found my palette of browns for next fall's line." She reached into her bag and pulled out a Polaroid—a close-up of a huge glass display case, inside of which were rows and rows of chocolate. "I came across this chocolate shop in Belgium. I mean, just look at those colors!"

"Great!"

She put the photo back in her bag and turned back to me. "How are you?"

"Fine."

As usual, she was not convinced.

"What's the matter?"

"Nothing," I said, desperately trying to relax the muscles in my face in case they had been fixed into an unwitting grimace. But it was too late. Her eyes were all over me, now.

"Not having any luck with the Bloomingdale's people?"

"No. They're fine. Lunch with three of them on Friday."

"The spread in *Vogue* fall through?"

I loved working for someone who had so much faith in me.

"No. The shoot's all set for next Monday."

"Then what is it?" She continued to examine my face with intense curiosity. Clearly she needed some reason to explain my mood, so I put it in terms I knew she could understand.

"I'm just pissed because I'm late and I really wanted to get in early so I could get started on everything."

This she could process. The desire to get one's hands into one's work—the frustration at being kept from doing so by some hapless force of nature—this she understood.

"I know. I cut my trip short because our nanny is sick and Arthur's in Los Angeles until tomorrow. I was supposed to get here hours ago, and I would have if the substitute nanny hadn't been late."

"What's wrong with the real nanny?"

"Mumps." She rolled her eyes skeptically, as if mumps— along with ulcers and pneumonia and cancer—were just another lame excuse in the pantheon of lame excuses that lazy people used to get time off from work.

"What about Marissa? Could she have been—"

"No. She was not exposed. She's fine." Suddenly Karen dropped her bags on the floor of the elevator and shoved her hands up under the black tunic, grabbing and pulling at the fabric around her waist.

"*These . . . fucking . . . leggings!*" she said over the snap of an elastic waistband. "I'm going to kill that fucking Annette. I told her these waistbands were too big. Look at this!" She tried to grab a fistful of puckered Lycra but was unsuccessful. Which didn't stop her. "With all this extra fucking material, I might as well ask three people to join me in here!"

The elevator doors opened, and in one swift, surprisingly graceful movement, she picked up her bags and stormed off toward her office.

Down the hall I could see Simon sitting peacefully at his desk, lazily twirling the ends of his hair around his index finger and then into his mouth, while enjoying what was obviously a personal phone call. But he hung up the receiver the second his otherworldly dog-hearing detected the telltale sound of her arrival—the *squeak-squish squeak-squish* of one Lycra thigh against the other—and dove toward her office. She slammed the door behind him, then a second later he reemerged and ran past me, his body bent at the forty-five-degree angle of indentured servitude.

"Where's that fucking Annette?"

I sat down at my desk and contemplated my encounter with Karen. Did she really believe her leggings were too big on her? Or was this just another flagrantly demented piece of her motherhood-denial puzzle? A denial puzzle that, for starters, included never ingesting anything in the office except for bottled water and Altoids and wearing Lycra leggings that were (usually) three sizes too small for her.

The idea that a woman with no pictures of her child anywhere in her office was a mother and I wasn't made me furious, then sad, but before I could indulge myself further in the deep dark vast well of injustice, I needed to deal with the work on my desk.

It was piled high with mail and message slips and press kits and invitations and newspaper and magazine ads in various stages of completion and all the other detritus that had accumulated the previous Friday afternoon, when I was out of the office for a lengthy lunch with the buyer from Bergdorf

Goodman. I slipped my jacket off and onto the back of my chair and tried to get my eyes to focus on all the paper on my desk, but I couldn't. I felt overwhelmed, the way I always did on Monday mornings.

I swiveled around in my chair and looked out the window.

From this perch on Fifty-seventh Street and Madison Avenue, I had an incredible view of the city south of midtown. Staring at the buildings and at all the teeny-tiny anonymous people with cars and buses swarming around them, I thought about the first time I came to New York to find a job, almost thirteen years ago.

How big everything seemed then. How big everything seemed still, though for very different reasons. Now, instead of facing merely the giganticness of the buildings and the giganticness of the egos inside them, I faced the pressure of my job; the endless sea of work that needed to get done every week and somehow did in spite of my waning interest and passion; how disconnected I felt I'd become in the midst of all this chaos and noise and perpetual motion. The veneer of glamour and allure that my career had once held for me—briefly, and without deep roots—had vanished long ago, and all that was left now was a persistent dread of the day that lay ahead.

I looked at my watch.

It was already eleven.

I picked up the phone and dialed the Pickle.

Naturally my sister answered.

"Hi."

"Hi."

"How's work?"

"Please."

"I saw the new ads you were telling me about. For the lingerie. The stuff looks great."

I glanced over at the color ads mounted on boards lined up on the floor along the windows—bras; panties; camisoles; teddies; silk; lace; satin; cotton, smooth or ribbed. If Malcolm had cared, I would have bought one of everything with my employee discount, the way every other single woman in the office had done months ago when the line first came in.

"I'll send you some," I said, searching my desk for a scrap of paper to write a note to myself on. "You want black or white or—"

"Don't bother."

"Why not?"

"I'm too fat for lingerie."

I stopped looking. "You are not." It was truly ridiculous— and frightening—how much time and energy we women spent discussing our collective distorted body image.

"I am, too."

"Stop it."

"You have no idea."

Ever since she and Paul had moved from Boston to Portland so he could be a full professor of American history at the University of Maine and she'd quit her graphic design job and had Nicole, all Lynn ever complained about was her alleged fat.

And her inability to form a complete sentence.

And her fear that she might never be able to hold her own again in a roomful of adults because she had nothing to wear except sweatpants and also because sometimes she suspected people thought she was a loser because she stayed home full-time with the Pickle and wore sweatpants all the time.

"Lingerie probably looks great on you, though."

"I wouldn't know."

Lynn paused, and I knew she was wondering if she should ask about Malcolm or not. But I knew she could tell that I wasn't in the mood to talk about him. She and my parents worried enough about my personal life—or seeming lack thereof—without my having to confirm their worries on a daily basis.

"Have you talked to Them?" I asked, changing the subject.

"I tried to, but they're packing."

"Packing?"

"For the Elderhostel."

"Another Elderhostel?" Why our parents couldn't stay home and take up golf like every other retired couple in the world was beyond us. Trips like these meant weeks of preparatory prepacking even before the actual packing—What suitcase should they take? Would they need dressy clothes or just casual? Could they get away with six pairs of shoes each or would they need the seven?—and because I was in the clothing business and was considered an expert on such matters, every trip required numerous phone calls to consult with me on these questions.

But my sister's perceived weight gain and my sexless sex life and my parents' packing problems weren't why I had called.

"So what's she wearing today?" I asked, getting down to the true purpose of our conversation.

This was a call I made every day, though not at any specific time—just at whichever point I needed to feel connected to a human being. Albeit a human being who was three and a half and still pooping in her Pull-Ups.

As usual, Lynn obliged my question with absolute earnestness. It had become as much a part of her day, I supposed, as changing diapers had, or cutting little tuna-fish sandwiches into tiny bite-size squares had, or whatever other weirdly specific request required her to indulge her daughter. Lynn had never become as hard and as cynical as I had; she accepted my obsession with Nicole without jealousy, without a sense of competition. What was hers was mine—clothes and books and record albums when we were growing up, and now her family. And while I felt guilty at times for placing this extra burden on her, of asking her to indulge me, too—another child, or simply a childish adult—I couldn't help myself.

I heard Lynn walk with the portable phone from the living room through the kitchen and into the back room where the Pickle, she told me, was sitting on the couch eating a waffle and watching *Barney*.

Ooof, I swooned, then waited impatiently for my report.

"Well, today she's wearing her denim shirt and her black leggings and . . ." For this she apparently had to bend over or lean over or do something strenuous sounding in order to get a better look at the rest of the outfit.

"*And . . . ?*" I prodded anxiously. This was the part I'd been waiting for, the part I always waited for: the shoes.

"And," my sister said finally, "her yellow jellies."

I closed my eyes: denim shirt, black leggings, yellow jellies.

The vision of her little feet inside those little yellow plastic shoes was sharp behind my closed eyes, until I opened them, reluctantly, a few seconds later.

"Thanks," I said, then sighed; an addict after a fix.

"Anytime. Talk to you tomorrow."

I hung up, wept, then called the airlines.

Thanksgiving was coming up.

It was time for another visit.

"SHE'S PREGNANT!" I said.

"Of course she's pregnant," Simon said.

"Light dawns over Marblehead," Renee added.

The two of them had come into my office several hours after my elevator encounter with Karen—with cigarettes and ashtrays and gigantic monolithic take-out cups of coffee—and Renee had started in on me immediately.

"I can't believe you didn't get it. You—the person who's obsessed with getting pregnant and having children. How could you not know?"

Through the glass windows of my office, I could see Karen through the glass windows of hers—she tucked her bone-straight fudge-colored hair behind both ears: cut and color courtesy of her appointment that afternoon with Frédéric Fekkai with whom she had a standing appointment every four weeks—and sat behind her big huge empty glass desk while Annette showed her a seemingly faulty zipper on a sample pant.

Like most Important People, her office was remarkably neat, bare of any evidence of actual work—files, papers, memos, message slips—containing only the requisite minimalist accoutrements befitting someone in her position: a huge television with built-in VCR for screening our latest ads and analyzing our runway shows; a cordless phone and three sleek black speaker units placed strategically around the office; a long white straight couch and two upholstered armchairs on an expanse of wheat-colored rug; an enormous high-backed ergonomically engineered futuristic leather swivel chair that, when she sat in it, dwarfed her and made her look like a child impersonating a boss; a laptop computer blinking and glowing on the low built-in credenza behind her; an open Palm Pilot in the center of the desk; and a bud vase full of deep-red grease pencils—her signature writing implement—that produced notes that looked as if they'd been written with lipstick.

"I don't know," I said, trying to come up with a Renee-proof excuse for my stupidity (even though I never could). "She'd been away for a while, so I thought she'd gotten carried away with the Belgian chocolate, but I guess I was just in denial."

"That's the understatement of the century."

"I don't think anyone else has figured it out either, but I've suspected for weeks," Simon said. "Ever since I noticed that extra finger or two of padding around the hips when she gave me a ride downtown recently. Sitting in the back seat with her, I couldn't seem to get our body parts not to touch, no matter how much I squirmed or how close I sat to the door. I felt rather—well, *suffocation* is the word that came to mind." A shiver seemed to undulate vertically through his wiry body, and he shook himself rid of it.

His reaction didn't surprise me, though I was sure it had less to do with Karen's weight than with the fact that Simon seemed to avoid close proximity to all human bodies. And while I was never quite sure about his sexual preference, I came to assume that whichever church he belonged to, he didn't much like going. Not that he'd have much opportunity anyway, given the fact that he lived with his mother—something he was surprisingly unashamed of at age twenty-seven. "My mother is a *saint,*" he'd say whenever her name came up—which was all the time, it seemed—genuflecting with his hands in the praying-tower position at his chest. "I re*vere* her." Which is what he could, on occasion, be overheard to say over the phone during the course of a normal business day about Karen, although when he said it about Karen, one couldn't help but detect a bit of a sneer.

I turned back to Renee, annoyed. I hated when other people knew things before I did. "Well, so, what, you figured it out immediately? Like, the morning after the fertilized egg implanted itself in her uterine wall?"

"No." She shifted in her chair, which made me immediately suspicious. Renee was never uncomfortable.

"How did you know, then? Did she tell you?" Even though I thought myself above petty jealousy, I felt myself get hot with indignation at the idea that Karen would confide in Renee and not me.

"No." She took a long drink from her coffee and played with the tassel on her gray suede loafer. "Arthur did."

Simon's neck craned so much, I thought he might pull a muscle. He scampered into the empty chair beside Renee as if we'd been playing musical chairs and the song had just stopped. "Arthur told you?"

She looked at each of us. "So?"

"So?" I mimicked. "Since when are you and Arthur such bosom buddies?"

"We're not bosom buddies," she mimicked back. "He was at the Dia Foundation fund-raiser a few weeks ago without Karen, and I asked him why she wasn't there."

"And he told you?" Simon assumed he was an equal partner in this interrogation, but I stared him down and he retreated to his chair.

"Well, he didn't mean to, but it just slipped out. You know how he is." She snapped her hand open and shut quickly—yap yap yap. "If I'd stood there long enough, which I didn't because he's so boring I would have killed myself, he would have told me her bra size."

Simon raised an eyebrow in disgust. "Which will, again, be ever increasing with each passing month."

"Of course, the minute he realized what he'd done, he begged me not to tell her that he'd told me. And not to tell anyone else about it, either."

I threw a paper clip at her, and it landed and stuck in her hair. "Like I'm just anyone."

"Look, you know how she is. She's never even brought Marissa into the office. She'd rip him a new asshole if she thought everyone was going to know she was pregnant before she was ready to announce it herself. She's the biggest control freak on the face of the earth."

"No, you're the biggest control freak on the face of the earth."

"Besides," she continued despite my baiting her, "there was something about Arthur's face when he told me how happy they were about it."

"They?"

"That's what he said. 'We are joyous.' "

While my head began to spin in disbelief at that incongruous thought—not to mention Renee's uncharacteristic sentimentality—Simon got up and paced back and forth behind her. He tapped his finger against his chin and spoke just above a stage whisper, like some B-level Method actor.

"I wonder how far along she is."

Renee and I ignored him.

"I wonder if they know yet what gender the child will be." He stopped and turned to us: so many questions, so little time. "I became quite friendly, last time around, with her obstetrician's assistant Tammy. Let's see how much information a messengered package containing KLNY champagne satin tap pants and a matching teddy will get us." Upon which he headed for the door.

Exit Simon.

"Barnaby Jones needs to get a life," Renee said, rolling her eyes at his departure. But when she saw the expression on my face, she could tell that my not knowing about Karen's pregnancy was only part of why I was upset. She walked around my desk, put an arm around my shoulders, and gave me a quick hug. "Don't worry," she said, hip-chucking me. "We'll get you a stupid baby. If I have to marry you off to some rich boring nebbish like Arthur, we'll get you a baby."

"FLEECE," I SAID to Amy the next day. "What's the deal with fleece? Everywhere you go: fleece, fleece, fleece."

The Baby Gap on Broadway and Sixty-eighth Street was

filled with the stuff. It was Saturday, around noon, and after we'd bought coffee and bagels, we made a pit stop there on our way back to her apartment. We'd gone in because she had to get a gift for a baby shower later that week, and I figured I'd cruise the sale racks for Nicole. Thousands of couples and baby carriages and strollers and children clogged the sidewalks on both sides of Broadway: it reminded me how lethal the Upper West Side was for single people. How Amy lived there without wanting to step out into traffic every weekend was beyond me.

"You're in the fashion business. What do you think?"

"What do I think? I think fleece is the sweatpants of the 1990s. I think it's the comfort food—the meat loaf—of clothes. It's insidious. It's a thick, bulky, nubby, ugly, unflattering fabric that no one looks good in, and I think it should be stopped. To her credit, Karen has been the one designer— the only designer—to resist fleece."

Amy scanned my face as if she were checking for imminent signs of apoplexy, then reconsidered the celadon fleece one-piece she was holding to purchase. She threw it back on the rack with irritation.

"*Thank* you."

She quickly picked out a nonfleece gift—a yellow waffle-cotton top and bottoms—and headed for the register. I waited on the sidewalk for her to come out, and it was then that she asked me what was wrong.

"Karen's pregnant again."

"Well, that explains it."

"Explains what?"

"Your diatribe on fleece back there." She smiled sympathetically, and we walked a block in silence. "When did you find out?"

"On Monday. I got on the elevator with her and suddenly realized that she was huge. I should have figured it out weeks ago, but as I told Renee, I guess I was in denial. Not to mention blinded by envy."

"I know. Two women in my department are pregnant and have the same due date: January tenth. I should take that week off. I'm so jealous, I can hardly get any work done."

An instant vision of two equally pregnant women popped into my mind—their stomachs bumping into each other like Tweedledum and Tweedledee—and before I could savor the image in my head, I caught myself.

"I just don't get it. I mean, here she is, a woman who never wanted children in the first place. Then she has one whom she never talks about, never brings to the office, never seems to be home long enough to enjoy—and now she's having another one. And according to Renee, who talked to Karen's husband, they're 'joyous.' I don't know. Maybe he was just projecting his joyousness onto her."

"Maybe. But maybe not."

"What do you mean?"

"Maybe she *is* joyous. Maybe she likes being a mother more than she lets on. Maybe she likes it more than she lets on to herself. I mean, from what you've told me about her, she doesn't sound like the most innately nurturing person in the world."

"She isn't."

"So maybe motherhood took her by surprise. You know, the way it takes men by surprise—men who have never wanted kids, who have never thought of themselves as daddy-types, but when they do have kids, they completely melt and become the most doting fathers in the world. Like my brother."

"Your brother was like that?"

"Until Isabel. Then he was a changed man."

I thought about the equation Amy had just offered, but it didn't exactly compute. After all, it wasn't like Karen brought

Marissa into the office every day and crawled around on all fours with her or got home early enough to crawl around on all fours with her there.

But then again, every mother is different. And maternal "saintliness" didn't necessarily produce sane children. Take Simon, for example.

"Speaking of Isabel," I said while we waited to cross Seventy-second Street, "how is she?"

A wave of rapture crossed Amy's face. She reached into her bag and pulled out a small piece of construction paper on which there were two or three smudges of color.

"Finger paint," she said.

Not to be outdone, at the next light I reached into my bag and produced a recent photo of the Pickle, all dressed up as a pilgrim for her little pre-preschool class pageant. Her fat cheeks and mop of hair underneath the black-construction-paper hat made me wish Thanksgiving was tomorrow, I missed her so much. But knowing how much she hated wearing hats, I could imagine the hellacious scene that had taken place when Lynn dressed her up that day. I pointed at the yellow dress and the yellow patent-leather ankle boots she wore.

"*Lello* is her favorite color."

We crossed Seventy-second Street and exchanged niece stories—what Isabel's favorite color was ("boo"); what both their favorite kind of cookies were ("chockit chip")—until Amy grabbed my arm and pulled me across the sidewalk to a newsstand kiosk.

"Hey, look," she said. "I want to show you something." We stood under the metal awning as she scanned the racks stuffed with magazines until she found what she was looking for. She reached for the November issue of *Glamour* and gave it to me—I knew it was in my office under a stack of other magazines I hadn't had the chance to open. "Arlene Schiffler has a column."

Arlene had been in our honors English class and had scored a perfect 800 on her verbal SATs—reason enough, certainly, for everyone to hate her. But when she got re-jected—*not even wait-listed!*—from Harvard for early admission, she'd come to class red-eyed and sniffling every day for a month. Now she was a freelance writer whose byline appeared too frequently for my taste in most of the women's magazines and who I'd occasionally run into over the years at various social events.

"Please." I was flipping through the magazine pages so hard, I almost tore a few out. "It's just another one of her stupid pseudojournalistic self-obsessed 'The Wonder of Me! Life As It's Happening to Me!' pieces. You know, 'My Irregular Pap Smear: 48-Hours of Fear and Loathing in Gynecology.' Or 'To Wax or Not to Wax: A (Hairless) Feminist Perspective.' She's always turning some inane beauty story into a fucking sociological epidemic."

"Well, now she's pregnant."

"By that cheeseball."

"What cheeseball?"

"That cheeseball husband of hers, that guy who's always outside reporting on something for MSNBC," I said before adding gratuitously: "The guy who wears the wig."

"He wears a wig?"

"Please," I said, as if everyone scrutinized the minutiae of people's features as much as I did. "His hair never moves. It never changes. 'Neither wind nor rain nor sleet nor snow . . .'" I let the sentence trail off unfinished. Then I gave the magazine back to Amy. "I can't handle this."

She flipped through it, trying to find the page she was looking for. "She's keeping a monthly diary. About what it's like to be pregnant. All the different stages; all the different emotions—everything." She turned the magazine around so I could read it now, too. "See? It's called 'Nine Months.'"

I read the first few sentences of the article. "This is repulsive."

"I know."

" 'No one can prepare you for the feeling you get when the stick turns blue. For me, it was a whirlwind of emotion: fear and joy and panic and selfishness and selflessness all fighting each other yet complementing each other like multiple personalities. And that was just in the first few seconds.' "

I poked Amy in the upper arm as if she were to blame for this waking nightmare.

"Did you read this whole thing?"

She nodded.

I read on: " 'If becoming pregnant in the safe womb of marriage was frightening, single motherhood must be completely terrifying. . . . It felt suddenly as if I were living inside another woman's body, though when I stared at my naked belly in the mirror that first night, I saw no discernible difference.' "

"God, I *hate* that word. *Belly.* And I can't talk about this anymore." Suddenly the incessant honking and cacophony of car alarms and police sirens and taxi doors slamming and people yelling felt unbearable; an assault I felt unprepared for and too vulnerable to withstand at that moment.

We turned onto Seventy-sixth Street and headed toward Amy's apartment. She had a corner two-bedroom on the seventeenth floor of a dark brick prewar building at the far side of West End Avenue. Her view faced north and east, and if you bent your head way back, you could see her windows from the street. But inside, later, looking out from those windows—looking up and down the sidewalks that threaded as far as the eye could see and thinking about what the future held and might not hold for me—it all looked so different than it had from down below; the way things always did from the outside looking in.

7

. . .

A FEW WEEKS later it became clear to anyone else who hadn't noticed that Karen was pregnant.

The proofs of the *Vogue* shoot for the February issue had just come in, and Renee and Annette and I were standing around Karen's desk admiring how great they looked. Simon had just brought in another case of water for Karen, which we'd helped ourselves to as if it were champagne—and just as we'd taken our first sips, Karen stopped swiveling in her chair.

Karen was always ill at ease in celebratory situations, so at first it seemed like this might just be one more time she was going to vacuum the joy out of the room. But when she put her hand to her mouth and bent forward and seemed to burp into the plastic lining of her wastebasket, we all looked at each other in horror.

Karen Lipps had barfed!

"Party's over," Karen said as she rushed past us to the ladies' room.

Even if Simon hadn't passed around a memo from Karen

the next morning tersely announcing her news, the rest of the office would have eventually figured it out, since she never seemed to get sick with anything—cold, flu, sore throat, food poisoning—and also since shortly thereafter the press had started noticing her weight, too.

Like the *New York Post,* which ran a mean little item on "Page Six" a few weeks later about how she'd been spotted tucking into a bowl of fettuccini with porcini mushrooms and cream sauce—reporting it with the requisite boldfaced subhead: "Karen 'Tipps' the Scales at Orso."

And then there was *The New York Observer,* which had simply started referring to her as "Moby Lipps" and "Karen Hipps."

"She'll probably fire me since I was the one who made her change her name to something that rhymes with all these fat words," I told Malcolm.

It was the Friday night after Karen's latest horrifying P.R. episode, and I was sitting at his kitchen table watching him cook us dinner. He had just transferred the saucepan on the front burner to the back burner so he could make room for another pot. This accomplished, he pulled a bag of mushrooms from the refrigerator and retrieved a large fennel bulb from a brown paper bag on the counter. This had become a familiar scene. Malcolm must have cooked me a hundred dinners and chopped a thousand vegetables in that kitchen in the time we'd been seeing each other.

I remembered the first night he'd made dinner over a year ago, when he'd asked me, as he was preparing the first of many elaborate salads, whether I liked fennel.

"Yes," I said.

"I love it," he said sardonically, his face and mouth spreading into a huge wry smile that made him look either strikingly handsome or criminally insane. I walked around to the counter where he was standing near the sink, slicing and peeling a vegetable I'd never really given much thought to before that moment. He cut a stalk in two and put a piece into his mouth and the other piece into my hand—a gesture I interpreted as being touchingly old-fashioned. Another man might have presumed to put it into my mouth, but not Malcolm. He seemed incapable of taking anything—and everything—for granted the way other people did. We chewed and crunched for a while, and then he smiled, and then I smiled, and then he cut another stalk in half, and we ate that, too.

Malcolm's apartment was a big, old, rambling set of rooms in one of those big, old, rambling Upper West Side apartment buildings where the elevator doors echo when they open and close and the hallways always smell of other people's cooking. He had lived there since the late 1970s, and the rooms still held what was left of those years when he had a family—walls and walls of books, all the furniture, and a few large abstract paintings. His wife, Jean, a social worker, had left behind almost everything, he told me, since she didn't think she could bear even the faintest traces of memory.

But he'd stayed on here, held on, hunkered down, as if hanging on to life itself—an instinct for survival so blind and so absolute, it had stunned him ever since.

"I don't know how I survived or why I wanted to," he'd said later that night, the first time I'd ever slept there.

"It's the life force," I said quietly, not knowing how else to explain the inexplicable will and strength needed to climb out of a hole so black and so deep.

"The life force," he repeated. "Is that what it is?"

His eyes bored into mine, and then he held me so tight, I thought my ribs might break.

I remember asking him that night why it was, besides the Prozac, that we didn't make love. What it was that made him so afraid.

"I don't think I could handle any more loss" was all he'd say when we'd talk about his past and how it was affecting us now. I came to understand that this was his way of not saying what he feared most—becoming attached to someone again:

You can't lose what you don't have.

And so he wouldn't have me.

Not like that, anyway.

Although he had me in other ways I thought were just as—or almost as—attachment producing:

Cooking for me.

Sleeping with me.

Marathon conversations that lasted, most weekends when we drove out to his house in Sag Harbor, well into the morning. Politics, history, fiction, food, movies we'd seen together—whatever the topic, he had an opinion on it and a desire to discuss it.

Like tonight's topic: Karen.

He hated Karen because of everything I'd told him. Plus he hated people like her on principle. Watching him move around the kitchen from stove to oven to cutting board, I could detect a glimmer of *Schadenfreude* in his eyes.

"What?" I asked.

"She's a pig," he replied.

"Hey, enough with the fat jokes. I'm already sick to my stomach."

"I don't mean pig in the sense of size or weight. I mean pig in the sense of how she behaves: pig as a person. She's always hated fat people, and now she's fat. She treats people like shit, and now she's getting treated like shit. What goes around comes around. Don't feel sorry for her. She doesn't deserve it."

He was right, and usually when he was right, when he defended me, when he made me feel like I wasn't crazy for feeling spent and empty after a stressful thankless week at work, I usually felt better. But for some reason that night was an exception. I was too weary—weary of all the mean-spiritedness, of all the nastiness, of all the obsessive emphasis on looks and weight and appearance that were endemic to the fashion business.

I sipped my water silently and wished Malcolm would stop his fucking chopping and stirring and cooking and put his arms around me, or grab me, or push me up against the wall and kiss me so hard it took my breath away. But that would never happen, I knew.

I could sit in that chair for hours and hours and hours the way I had so many times during the year we'd been seeing each other, and neither of us would do anything of the sort. We would eat dinner and move into the living room after-ward and talk until it got very late and we were exhausted, and then we would finally go to sleep together. Most times, that was enough. Or better than nothing. That's what I would tell myself those nights in the dark when I lay awake next to Malcolm.

But sometimes it wasn't enough, and it wasn't better than nothing. Sometimes being with him made me feel lonelier than being alone.

I got up to set the table, taking the dishes out of the cabi-nets, then the silverware out of the drawer, and then the glasses out of the dish drainer. We moved in parallel orbits around each other the way we always did when we were in his place, or my place, or when we went out for breakfast or dinner or to see a movie. We were together but separate. There were times when I would feel one of those compass points more acutely than the other, as I did that night, when all I could feel was the separation.

It seemed like our situation would have been so easy to remedy. So easy to break the force field that kept us apart by simply walking through it—a kiss when I stepped into his apartment or he into mine instead of just a nod or a half smile, as if the other had been there all along; an embrace before we left each other in the morning; or a thousand other simple gestures through which two people communicate affection and feeling and intimacy without speaking.

But we did not do those things—did not touch or embrace or kiss unless we were in bed, and even then our physical vocabulary was limited, truncated, as if there were a line we could come upon but not cross. And though I often wanted to, I rarely pushed the limits of our tacit understanding; did not often challenge the official verbal language of our relationship with sexual language. I was afraid that I would, once again, come up against his silence and rejection. It was simply too difficult to feel the panic rising through his muscles, to accept the impulses and instincts that I believed still existed in his mouth and his hands and his body shutting down and short-circuiting, until my touch or embrace or kiss had been neutralized, contained.

Had there been no physical attraction between us, had our relationship been clearly a platonic one, things between us would have been easier; the boundaries of our interaction would have been more defined; desire and possibility would have been removed from the equation resulting in a friendship—no more, no less.

Sometimes when we were together I would try to suppress my feelings—try not to want what I might never get from him—and yet those synapses kept firing. During the split seconds when desire and need and longing converged, I was led, despite my conditioning and my misgivings, to try again.

I put my glass down and crossed the kitchen floor to where he was standing, his back to me, facing the sink. Over the sound of the water running, it seemed he was unaware of me there, so close. I stopped, not sure if I should retreat, and for that instant I felt the familiar confusion and paralysis set in, as if, like a stroke victim, I no longer remembered how to execute the simplest movements that had always been so automatic. And just when I thought I might lose my nerve completely, I willed myself to move forward and slip my hands under his arms and around his waist and lean my forehead against his back.

He reached to shut the water faucets off, and then his hands, wet from washing the potatoes, covered my hands. Our fingers locked, and I closed my eyes.

A minute or so passed before he loosened his grip and turned around. My eyes welled up with tears, and I tugged at the rolled-up sleeves of his shirt.

"I'm sorry," he whispered. His arms stayed around me, and his hands rested just above the small of my back, and I could feel his chin against my forehead. I knew my disappointment about this part of our relationship tore him up and shamed him, and I wished again that there could have been a way for me to communicate desire without disappointment.

"I wish—I just wish we could—"

"I know," he whispered again. "I'm sorry."

"Is it me?" I asked, which is what I always asked at moments like this.

"It's not you." He let out a heavy breath. "It's not you."

"Then what is it?"

"I don't know."

I considered asking again if he would go to see someone—a shrink, a therapist—someone we could see together—who could help him untie the knot that was strangling him—or even if he would go back to his psychopharmacologist who could try to switch him to a different antidepressant—but that had never really worked.

He'd only say maybe, and later, days later or weeks later, it would become clear that he hadn't made any calls, and then the subject would again be dropped.

I put my head on his shoulder and then turned my face into his neck, to where his tie would have been if he hadn't ripped it from his collar the second he'd gotten home the way he always did. He smelled like soap and clean laundry and garlic and onions, and I closed my eyes again, feeling my eyelashes blink against his throat, and I wished we were just a normal couple—just two normal people sharing a normal moment together before dinner.

"This can't be good for you," he said quietly.

I lifted my head and looked into his eyes.

"You should be with someone else. Someone younger. Less complicated. Less damaged. You shouldn't be wasting your time with someone like me."

"But I don't want someone else," I said. "I want you."

"I don't give you anything."

"Yes, you do." I thought of the comfort and safety and closeness I'd felt with him and that I'd come to need and to rely on so much the past year. The possibility I might lose even that terrified me. "You *do.*"

"I don't give you the important things. I can't," he said, "give you the other things. Things you need, things you want. Things you deserve to have."

I wiped my eyes again. "It's okay," I whispered, though I knew better. I knew this relationship, as it was, wasn't good for me, and I knew, once again, that I was rationalizing the lack of our physical intimacy.

"No. It's not okay. You should want those things. A young attractive woman should be touched. Should have an intimate relationship. Don't extinguish those parts of yourself like I have. They're too important. Too precious. And once they're gone, they're gone for good."

I pulled at his arms under his shirt cuffs. "But we could try," I said. "I could help you."

He shook his head.

"I could," I said. "I could bring you back."

He shook his head again. "People don't come back from where I've been."

"Yes, they do. If they want to, they do." I stared at him, wishing my eyes could bore holes in him, tunnels through which my words could enter his body and take root. "Don't you want to? Don't you want to try?"

"I don't know. I don't know if there's anything left of me. I don't know if I have the courage. Or the strength."

"But I'll help you," I said, raw pleading in my voice. "I'll *help* you."

He met my eyes, and when he did, I could see the defeat give way slowly to confusion, then bafflement, and then to something else—hope? trust?—that I'd never seen in him before.

"But why?" he said. "Why would you even want to?"

"Because."

"Because why?" His hands tightened their grip on my arms, and it felt almost like he might shake the answer out of me.

"Because—I love you."

The words came out before I could stop them, before I even knew they were there, as if a bright light had been turned on in a dark room and made them visible. I had never said those words first, had never been willing to risk so much up front, but now that I had, I felt brave suddenly, and alive—as if the sheer power of truth and will and faith could save us both.

"How can you love me?" he whispered.

I shrugged. "I just do."

"But why?"

"Because I believe in you. Because I believe you're still in there."

Pain and disbelief and relief laced through the lines of his face. "How can you love someone who might not exist? How can you believe in something you've never seen?" He put his hands gently on either side of my face and held them there. "How can you be so unafraid?"

"So unafraid of what?"

He searched my eyes for the word. "Of disappointment."

"Because I want this to work. You're different from anyone I've ever known. You have grit—sheer grit—to have survived everything you've survived. And because of that—because you understand pain—I trust you. More than I've trusted any man."

"But I can't promise you anything. I don't know how long it will take for me to get better. And I don't even know if—I can't guarantee that I'll ever get better." He paused. "That way."

"I think you will."

"What if I don't, though? You'll have wasted your time for nothing."

"I'm willing to take that chance. I'll wait, if you want me to."

He leaned his forehead against mine and clenched his jaw.

"Yes. Wait for me," he finally answered. "Please wait for me."

8

. . .

LATE THE FOLLOWING Thursday night, my parents
called. Thanksgiving was in two weeks and they were packing for the trip up to Maine, where we were all meeting to
spend the holiday together. But they were also packing for
an Elderhostel in the Berkshires, to which they were going
straight from Lynn's. Packing for one trip was bad enough,
but packing for two—one immediately following the other
in two similar but slightly different climates without time to
go home first and unpack before repacking!—was unheard
of. I could just imagine my father's flow charts and clip-
boards and checklists (he'd been a mechanical engineer
before retiring) and my mother's increasing fear that four
suitcases would not be enough (she'd grown up in the
Depression).

"I can't believe you're going to another Elderhostel," I
said. "I feel like you just came back from one."

"We didn't just come back," my mother said. "We came
back in October."

"Over a month ago," my father added.

I closed my eyes and rubbed my temples. They were in stereo, on the speakerphone, talking way too loud as usual. "It just seems kind of excessive."

"It's not excessive. We like to learn."

"We're active people. Just because we're retired doesn't mean we—"

"Have no interest in learning."

"I think it's great that you like to learn. But maybe you could learn someplace closer to home. You know, so you wouldn't have to keep traveling. And packing."

And torturing me.

"But we like to travel. And packing isn't such an ordeal."

"We're getting it down to a science."

I laughed out loud. "Have you broken the four-suitcase barrier yet?"

"We're going to try to get away with three this trip," my mother said with pride.

Through the receiver I heard papers rustling and my father moving around. "Well, not if you count the presents for Nicole. And the carry-on shoulder bags we keep in the backseat. And the shoes that won't fit in the—"

"Don't be so technical."

"I wasn't being technical, I was trying to be honest."

Whatever.

"Anyway, what's the educational focus of this Elderhostel?"

"Jewish music," my mother said.

"Jewish music again?"

What was so endlessly fascinating about klezmer music that could sustain studying it for an entire week?

"What do you mean, 'again'?"

"Didn't you just go to one on Jewish music?"

"No. The last one was on Jewish literature."

"And the one before that was on Jewish films?"

"Israeli films," my mother corrected.

It was all starting to come back to me. The literature trip was in northern California in the fall; the film trip had been in Miami in June. How could I ever forget the endless summer/autumn weather-related questions; the climate questions; the casual-versus-dressy questions? I couldn't help wondering whether their constant Elderhosteling would be less annoying to me if they studied some subject unmodified by the adjective *Jewish,* but I doubted it. They'd still need to know what to pack for an ashram.

It didn't take long for me to dispense with this trip's winter-related and general clothing dilemmas ("Yes to the L.L. Bean wool-lined field coats *and* to the down parkas"; "No to the two separate dressy outfits, since you probably won't even wear the one"; "Only one pair of Rockport walking shoes each"). But that was a mixed blessing. Being done with them only meant they could focus on me. Which I dreaded.

My father got off the phone, and then it was just my mother and me, now.

"So?" she asked.

"So . . . what?"

"So . . . what's new?"

"New? Nothing's new."

Nothing was ever new.

"*Nothing's* new?"

No man? No marriage proposal? No plans for the future?

"That's right."

And when something is new, you'll be the first to know.

"Oh."

"You sound disappointed." I knew she was just curious, just trying to figure out if I was happy or not, the way any other mother would—but I couldn't help being defensive. There was always some sort of judgment in her questions—

or maybe I only heard it that way—and I was tired of always feeling like I had to justify myself and my life to her. It was something I'd felt compelled to do ever since I was a child, and I'd never outgrown it. If I ever had children of my own, I vowed I would never make them feel judged. How predictable.

"I'm not disappointed. I'm just wondering if we're ever going to meet your friend."

"What friend?"

"Malcolm."

Malcolm?

"Now's not a very good time."

"Will there ever be a good time?"

"I don't know."

"I mean, you've been seeing him for a while now, and we still haven't met him. We were just thinking that it would be nice if he came for Thanksgiving, that's all."

"Yes, it would be nice." And I had to admit, I would have loved for him to meet my sister and my Pickle.

"So will you ask him?"

"Sure, I'll ask him."

But I didn't have to. I knew he wouldn't come.

LIKE EVERY OTHER normal person in the world, Amy was dreading the holidays. Since I was too, especially after the previous evening's conversation with my parents, we felt we needed to talk each other down off of our respective ledges. Friday night after work, she came over to my apartment, and we ordered dinner in. When our sushi arrived, we sat on the floor in the living room on opposite sides of the coffee table and ate like pigs.

"I hate them," she said.

"I know. Me, too."

"Does anyone like them?"

"I don't know. Probably not."

"There must be some people, somewhere, who like them."

"You think?" I went into the kitchen and returned with a flask of sake I'd heated up and two small ceramic cups.

"There has to be. People who are normal. Who aren't depressed. People for whom Thanksgiving and Christmas are just pleasant painless meals to be shared with family."

"You mean, like people for whom a cigar is just a cigar?"

"And a holiday is just a holiday."

I tried to picture who would fit her description, but I kept coming up with the same visual: Teletubby-type aliens with those metal antennae on springy metal coils attached to their heads.

Amy eyeballed me, as if she were waiting for an actual answer. "Maybe people in the South like the holidays. Or people in the Midwest."

"People who wear fleece, you mean."

"Don't start in on that again."

"Sorry."

"I'm serious. I mean, why can't we be like that?"

"Be like what?"

"The kind of people who like holidays."

The same visual as before appeared in my mind—only this time she and I were the Teletubby aliens with the boinging antennae. "Because we're not."

"But why can't we be?"

"Because. We're not wired like that. We're too . . ."

"Too what?"

"Too *complex,*" I said, heavy on the sarcasm.

"I don't know," she said. "Sometimes I think that's bullshit. Like we just overcomplicate everything."

"You mean, that we choose to be miserable?"

"Yes. And that we could, just as easily, choose not to be miserable."

I thought a minute. "Positivity," I said, feeling quite clever about having thought of this new word, "instead of negativity."

"Exactly. Positivity."

I moved my empty containers away and pushed back from the coffee table to lean up against the couch. "Well, feel free to pursue positivity if you want to, but I'm going to stick with negativity. It's worked just fine for me so far."

"No, it hasn't."

"Yes, it has."

"What's it gotten you?"

"Who says I've wanted anything?"

She looked away, and when she did, I knew it was time for me to ask her what this whole preamble was leading up to.

"I'm just dreading going to Chicago to meet Will's family."

"So why are you going?"

"Because he invited me. And because I'm supposed to be grateful that after a year and a half, he's finally letting me meet them. Or letting them meet me. At least you don't have to deal with this shit."

"Oh, *right,*" I said, and laughed. "One of the many benefits of being involved with someone whose family has been decimated."

Amy seemed far more frustrated about her relationship with Will than she had been when we first met—or rather, frustrated with his neurotic commitmentphobia that kept stopping her at checkpoints all along the way. And to make matters worse, the December issue of *Glamour* was out and apparently burning a hole in her bag. She reached for the magazine and dumped it on the table, and it fell open where a giant paper clip had marked Arlene Schiffler's latest diary entry.

"Month two," she said.

I glanced down at the page and scanned a half column of text. This month's focus? Morning sickness. How original.

She had already finished the flask of sake and had come back from the kitchen with a refill. She fidgeted on the floor across from me, and I wondered, for the second time that night, what was really bothering her.

So I asked.

She sipped her drink and smiled the way she usually smiled when she was happy. Only she wasn't, I realized suddenly, when I saw her eyes well up with tears.

"What," I said softly. "What's the matter?"

She covered her eyes with her hands tightly, then took them away, wiping her lids as she did.

"I can't stand it anymore."

"Stand what?" I looked down at the magazine and wondered if that was what she was talking about. "This?" I regarded it disdainfully and pushed it away across the table.

She nodded yes, then no. "Arlene's column. The two women in my office. Karen. Everyone's pregnant all over the place all of a sudden, and I want to be, too. God, I hate this time of year. November. My mother died in November."

"I'm sorry," I whispered. No wonder she hated the holidays. As she wiped her eyes again and played absently with one of her chopsticks, I couldn't help feeling incredible guilt over my contentious conversation with my mother the night before. At least I still had a mother to disapprove of me.

"I want to be married. I want a family," she said finally. "My own family. I'm sick of always being a guest at my father's house or my brother's house. I'm sick of always being the one unmarried person at the end of the table—the loser—who everyone assumes can't cook a turkey because she doesn't have anyone to cook one for."

I made a face, and she laughed a little.

"Okay, so they're right about the turkey. But you know what I mean."

Of course I knew what she meant.

While I was salivating at the thought of my impending Pickle-time in two days, I was dreading the reminder that when it came to holidays and other family get-togethers, I was, as Amy had just described, the odd person out; the perpetual adolescent; the one who always came alone and was sent home with enough toaster-oven-reheatable leftovers to feed a dormitory full of women like me. Reentry into my adult life always took time, not to mention the emotional setback that lingered, it seemed, for weeks after.

But I wasn't an adolescent. And I didn't feel like one.

"Look, I want a family, too," I said.

She shook her head. "Sometimes I think it's never going to happen."

"Of course it's going to happen," though I wasn't sure it was going to happen with Will.

"I keep going over the future trajectory of our relationship, and the math doesn't add up. Look," she said. "He's thirty-eight, and I'm almost thirty-six. It's taken a year and a half for him to introduce me to his family. He's no closer to wanting to get married than he was when I met him. He's looking for a new apartment—a cheaper apartment, if you can believe it—cheaper than the one he's in, which is already incredibly cheap since he can't afford anything else—and there's been no mention about us moving in together. Not that I'd even want to, since I think living together is a huge fucking myth and since it would definitely waste another three years, after which he'd probably dump me anyway." She shrugged her shoulders, and the big smile came back, only this time without the tears. "He's broke. He doesn't have a job-job because he's supposed to be working on his dissertation. But he's not working on his dissertation because he's so depressed about how shitty his life is. And any day now he's going to really start resenting me because I make more money than he does."

Malcolm was suddenly starting to look pretty good by comparison.

"So what should I do?" she asked. "Should I dump him?"

While I silently searched for a noncommittal answer, she continued.

"But I don't want to dump him. I'm in love with him. And I don't know if I can go back to being alone again. I just don't think I can do it again."

I thought about what she'd said tonight and what I'd said tonight and about what we'd talked about every single time we'd gotten together: my Pickle and her Pumpkin, and our desire for commitment—Amy wanting one from Will and me wanting one from Malcolm. And yet maybe we were the ones who had to commit to what we wanted: children. I looked over at the magazine, squished at the end of the table like a big dead bug, then took a deep breath.

"Maybe we should give ourselves a deadline."

"What kind of deadline?"

"A deciding deadline. A set amount of time that we'll use to come to a decision, one way or another, about what we're going to do."

"Do about what?"

"About having kids."

"You mean, by ourselves."

"Maybe. Presumably—in my case anyway, given what I'm working with. At least you and Will have sex. You're *way* ahead of me in the anything-is-possible department."

"By ourselves how, though?"

"I don't know. The way other women who are in the same position as we are do it."

"With turkey basters? Like lesbians?"

"No. Not with turkey basters. You know, like sperm banks. Or by accident. Or the direct approach, by asking someone to—"

"To donate?"

"I guess."

"Who would you ask?"

"I have no idea. I haven't even thought about it." Which wasn't a complete lie. The idea of asking Malcolm had crossed my mind once or twice, but in the past I'd always dismissed it out of hand. Until recently it had seemed too far-fetched, too disconnected from reality—the reality of our relationship and of Malcolm's state of mind. But now that we'd had some kind of emotional breakthrough, I wondered if I myself shouldn't exercise some positivity.

She sat back in her chair and considered my proposal.

"I could just stop using my diaphragm," she said, "only I'm not sure I want to do it alone. I'm not sure I even could do it alone—emotionally or financially."

"I'm not saying we'll have to. We're still only thirty-five. And I'm not sure I want to do it alone or could do it alone, either. I'm just saying we should start investigating it. So when the time comes—when our gum-ball machines are on their last eggs—we'll have a backup plan."

She looked at me and said nothing, but I could tell she wanted me to go on, since having a plan—any plan about anything at all—made us feel like we had control of our futures instead of waiting for them to pass us by.

"Let's say we give it nine months," I said matter-of-factly, as if I were talking about a diet, or a fitness plan, and not genetic reproduction. "Just like Arlene Schiffler's column. Nine months from now"—I counted on my fingers and

mouthed the names of the months from November on—
"by August—by *Labor* Day, let's say"—and I paused to smile
goofily at my stupid but remarkably apt target-month pun—
"we'll each come to a decision. Either to do it and how to
do it. Or to not do it."

"Or," Amy said, "to keep waiting."

AFTER AMY LEFT, I packed my black nylon overnight bag
and took a taxi up to Malcolm's apartment so we could leave
early the next morning for Sag Harbor. We went out to his
house most weekends, and while we tried to leave Friday
night, we'd leave early on Saturday morning if either of us
had something to do the night before, or if we didn't feel
like rushing. Like this time.

I liked Malcolm's house, a yellow clapboard built in the
late 1800s. It stood on Bridge Lane in Sag Harbor, and
despite how close it was to the center of town, the street was
remarkably quiet.

The house was small—four rooms downstairs and two
bedrooms upstairs—with a screened-in porch in the back
and a small open porch in front, but it was the kind of house
that somehow seemed bigger from the inside than it looked
from the outside. Not that he would have needed more
space. It was just him alone there after Benjamin died and
Jean left. For years, he told me, before he cleared out
Benjamin's old things and turned the second bedroom into a
study, he used to sit in that little room in the dark, all night
sometimes. That was when he still drank. A few years ago he
bought an old refectory table to use as a desk and had bookshelves built on every wall, and now and then on the weekend, in between cooking or reading or talking, I'd see him
go in there, bend over the desk to put a newspaper clipping
into a file folder or scour the shelves for a book he was look-

ing for. But as far as I knew, he hadn't been able to write anything for five years. Not since Benjamin's death.

The taxi let me out at the corner of Ninety-sixth and Broadway, and I walked into the lobby of Malcolm's building and waved past the doorman. Malcolm was expecting me and had left his door unlocked and open a crack in anticipation of my arrival. He was just coming out of the kitchen when I stepped into the foyer and shut the door behind me.

"How was dinner?" he said, reaching for my coat and hanging it in the hall closet.

"It was okay."

"Where'd you go?"

"We didn't. She came over, and we ordered in."

He started for the living room, expecting me to follow.

"So what's new with Amy?"

Malcolm had never met her—he was uncomfortable meeting new people, as he dreaded answering their questions—but he liked the sound of her from everything I'd told him. He thought she sounded unpretentious and sincere, and after I told him that her mother had died a year ago, he seemed to soften toward her even more.

I positioned myself on the couch, and he sat on the armchair across from me.

"She's frustrated," I said.

"Frustrated about what?"

"She wants to get married and have kids already, and it's just not happening yet."

Well, he *asked*.

"What's the deal with Smarty Pants?"

Malcolm almost never called anyone by their real name, especially someone who sounded as immature as Will, from what I'd told him—and especially someone with too much formal education, which he found highly suspect.

"Nothing. I mean, nothing new. She's going to Chicago for the holiday to meet his family, finally."

He shook his head. "Tell her she should get another boyfriend," he said. "Because it doesn't sound like it's going to happen with this one."

He was right, I knew, but I regretted bringing the subject up anyway. My wanting children and him not had never been a positive conversation point for us, given how fraught the subject was to begin with.

We had talked about it several times, oddly enough, given the fact that we didn't have sex—talked about it the way we talked about most things: intellectually, hypothetically, in the abstract. One unusually chilly night in late August, he asked me for the first time if I wanted children, and I hadn't thought to tell him anything but the truth.

"That's good," he'd said, as if I'd just told him I wanted to spend a year in Italy studying art. "You should have them. It's the most important experience you can have in life, and you shouldn't miss out on it."

I was hurt that he'd said *I* should have them—it's an experience *I* shouldn't miss out on—making it clear that our lives were destined to divide and separate and that he'd already accepted it as fact—and maybe even with relief. His words and his tone were dispassionate and objective, and because it had stung me to hear him sound so distant, I decided to turn the question back on him.

"Would you ever want to have another child?"

He'd thought a minute before answering.

"I did, when Benjamin was still alive. I'd always wanted a daughter. But after he—" He paused, and I saw the muscles in his jaw tighten. "No. To give you the short answer to your question, I don't want to have another child."

The longer answer wasn't that hard to figure out—how he couldn't replace Benjamin and didn't want to; how he couldn't bear the thought of something bad happening again. It was easy to connect those dots.

"It's too much baggage to bring to the table," he'd said. "It would be unfair to impose that burden on a child—to make them afraid of life because I'm afraid of death." He had looked at me then, to see my reaction, and because I wanted him to leave the subject open, even just a little so it wouldn't be sealed shut forever, and because I was still feeling stung from his earlier remark, I decided to challenge him on it.

"It's less about how it would affect a child and more about you. About your fear. About what it would mean for you to risk something as big as that again." He said nothing, so I pressed on. "But maybe in time the fear would go away. Maybe if you felt joy again—if you felt life again—it would recede. Recede enough to become manageable. Enough so you could learn to live with it."

"I don't know if that kind of fear is manageable. If it's something I could learn to live with. I mean, what's more frightening than losing a child?"

"Never having one."

We'd left it there that night, and I hadn't thought about the discussion again until now—until he'd said that Amy should find someone else because she wasn't going to get what she wanted from Will—and I couldn't help but feel his words were some kind of veiled message for me, too.

"Are you trying to tell me something?" I asked, my throat constricting as I tried to get the question out.

He looked confused. "What do you mean?"

"I mean, is the advice you're giving Amy the advice you're trying to give me? Are you trying to tell me I should find someone else, too?"

"That's not what I meant."

"But is it what you think?"

"I think you need to figure out what you want."

"I want you," I said. *You healed. Fixed. Normal.*

"But you also want children."

"I want both."

"I can't give you both. And I don't know if I could live with myself knowing that I was depriving you of something so important. I care about you too much to do that to you."

"So what are you saying?" I asked. Until now, I'd thought we'd been making progress, getting closer—but maybe not.

"I'm saying that you need to decide which you want more."

"That's some choice." I turned away. He was right, and I knew it.

"Yes, it is. But it's a choice you have to make, and one that shouldn't be made by default. If you do that, you'll regret it for the rest of your life."

He came over and sat down on the couch and put his arm around me, and we sat there for a few minutes, in silence, in stillness. When he reached for my hand, I held it tightly.

"Come on. It's late," he whispered. "Let's go to bed."

THE SKY WAS still an opaque blue-gray when we left early that morning. I didn't sleep during the drive, and neither of us said much, save for an occasional comment about an errant driver or the clouds giving way to clear sky. I felt numb somehow—as if everything with Malcolm had to be examined and reexamined. I knew I would soon have to make decisions I had long avoided making—decisions I didn't want to make because in the process of making them, I knew, something would inevitably have to be lost.

Usually going to Malcolm's beach house on the weekend was the perfect antidote to the established rhythm of our week together—the leisurely conversations about my work or his teaching while we sat on the screened-in porch reading the

Sunday papers. Packing up to go, loading his old Volvo station wagon in the garage below his building with our bags and our books and our magazines and, for Malcolm, always a dog-eared cookbook or a fistful of recipes clipped from the *Times* for some new soup or curry or stew he wanted to try—heading crosstown and through the Midtown Tunnel and then out to the Long Island Expressway at dusk as night was falling, I would feel something deep inside of me relax. Malcolm's quiet house, the smell of saltwater that blew in from the harbor, the easy hours of being together—seductive as narcotics—were close at hand.

Malcolm always drove, and sometimes if we were on the road at night, I'd fall asleep in the passenger seat next to him. I'd lean my head against the window and feel the smooth steady stream of heat or air conditioning coming through the vents depending on the season or the weather, listening to the low hum of the engine and the static-filled sound of the radio playing NPR or something classical turned down low so it wouldn't wake me. Those times I'd open my eyes and see him in silhouette, staring at the darkened road ahead of us. I'd turn to him, and he'd turn to me, and for a brief instant I'd feel a wave of absolute calm, of connection, of something that, while unnamed early on, I would later come to know as love. Alone in the car with him, in the quiet of that moment, with only the dim yellow lights of the dashboard to break the darkness, I'd feel safe, and certain, though safe from what and certain of what I didn't know, and before I could form a question or a thought, his eyes would return to the road, and soon mine would, too. And while we never talked during those moments, the rest of the ride would be different. A feeling, a current, had passed between us, and like everything else that was silent and invisible with us, it left us each somehow changed.

It was just past eleven when we got to his house, and some of the tension I'd been feeling had lifted. I carried the bag of vegetables we'd bought at a roadside stand into the kitchen, while Malcolm dropped our bags in the front hall next to the stairs. A few envelopes and a weekly supermarket circular from the local IGA were scattered, as usual, on the floor under the mail slot. But when Malcolm picked them up, I saw the telltale muscles in his jaw tense.

"What is it?" I asked, leaning lightly against his right arm. From there I could see it was a handwritten note—with lively script—a woman's script—covering the creamy white stationery.

Malcolm looked at me absently, then refolded the note and put it, along with the rest of the unopened mail, on the side table. "It's a note from Ted and Florence. Inviting me to have Thanksgiving with them."

"Who are Ted and Florence?" I asked.

"Ted and I were at the *Times* together. He is—or was, actually—one of my closest friends."

"So what happened?" I asked, following him. "I mean, why aren't you friends anymore?"

Malcolm unpacked the vegetables into the refrigerator in silence, then shut the door and leaned against it, his arms folded tightly across his chest. He was wearing a faded navy T-shirt and over it an old blue plaid flannel shirt that had two buttons missing at the bottom. "They have a son, Sam, who was—who is—the same age as Benjamin. As Benjamin would have been. The two used to play together out here"—he motioned his head toward the kitchen window and the small patch of grass in the backyard—"and in the city. After Benjamin died, we stayed in touch for a while. Jean and Florence and Ted and I would have dinner occasionally during the week in the city, or out here on a weekend once in a while. But it was never the same. Especially after Jean left me. I couldn't—" He turned away from the window and looked down at the floor. "I couldn't handle seeing Sam. I couldn't help thinking how unfair it was, how—" He shook his head and held his hand, palm open, over his mouth. "I just couldn't handle it."

"I can understand that."

He looked at me. "You can?"

"Of course I can," I said softly. "Of course it would be hard for you, painful for you, to see him. It would be torture." I looked at the kitchen window, then remembered the pictures of Benjamin I'd seen in Malcolm's apartment— mouth wide open, full of baby teeth, lips wet with mischief and glee—and tried to imagine the voices of two little boys playing in the summer dusk. "When was the last time you saw them?"

"Ted and Florence?" He looked past me, thinking. "Oh, I don't know. Two years ago. Maybe three. Someone, I can't remember who now, had a cocktail party out here during the summer, and they were there. Not Sam, of course. I haven't seen him since—since whenever. They've always kept in touch, though, or tried to, anyway—Christmas cards, birthday cards—my birthday and Ted's are two days apart. But this invitation, inviting me for Thanksgiving"— he shrugged, seemingly at a loss—"that's what we used to do. That's what we did for five years—spend it together out here, at our house one year, then at theirs, switching off every year. I'm surprised they've asked me now."

"Maybe they think enough time has passed."

"Enough time has passed for what?"

"That maybe you'll be able to handle it now. Handle seeing them. I'm sure they understood why you couldn't see them all this time. Maybe now they think reconnecting would do you good. Do you all good."

He seemed momentarily lost in thought, lost in the

past—in a past I had not been a part of and would never completely understand no matter how much I tried to. The death of a child—of his child—was something I didn't know about. I crossed the kitchen and put my arm around his waist, then leaned up and kissed him lightly on the throat. And when he didn't respond, I moved away slowly, back out of the kitchen and into the hallway, into the present; my present.

A WEEK LATER, as I waited at LaGuardia for my flight to Portland to board, I called Malcolm to say good-bye, but his machine picked up instead. He hadn't yet decided whether he would spend Thanksgiving with Ted and Florence and Sam, or whether he would accept an invitation from some other friends in Montauk instead. I'd asked him if he wanted to come to Maine with me, but as expected, he'd declined, and I'd left him at his apartment that Wednesday morning with a heaviness that began to abate only when I pulled into Lynn and Paul's driveway four hours later and saw my Pickle's face pressed up against the glass of the living-room window, waiting for her Auntie LaLa.

9

· · ·

EARLY THE NEXT morning, in bed, the Pickle put her hands on my face and then pulled on my nose. We always slept together when I visited, and usually I'd wake up first, too excited by the chance to see her perfect little face—almond eyes closed, wide mouth slightly turned upward, big fluff of dark curly hair exploding on the pillow—so deep in sleep.

I opened my eyes, hugged her to me, then put my face between her neck and shoulder and swooned from the sweet softness of her skin.

"Auntie LaLa. Auntie *LaLa*." Her tone got increasingly insistent with every second I kept her trapped in my embrace. "We have to get up."

Reluctantly I released her from my clutches and got in a quick nose kiss. "Why?"

"Because we *have* to."

"Because we have to why?"

She pulled on my nose again. "Auntie LaLa. We *have* to get up because we *have* to get up."

Clearly I wasn't going to get more of an answer than that, so I stopped asking. Sun was coming through the bedroom window as I marveled at all the dolls and games and toys and books neatly arranged on her bookshelves. I heard voices coming from downstairs and smelled coffee and turkey wafting up from the kitchen. Suddenly I was ravenous. I pulled on my jeans and a white long-sleeved thermal underwear shirt and a pair of thick gray rag wool socks while Nicole tried (unsuccessfully) to dress herself in a pair of black leggings and a pink angora cardigan. After finishing what she'd started, I got on my hands and knees to survey the huge expanse of shoes in her closet—mostly ones that I'd bought and shipped and heard about during my daily conversations with Lynn. It wasn't long before I spied the yellow jellies in the corner.

Oooooeuf!

"How about these?" I said, reaching for them.

She shook her head. "I don't want to wear those."

I let a beat go by, then went back into the closet. "How about these?" This time I offered the pair of bright green suede Hush Puppies I'd bought on sale on Madison Avenue.

She shook her head again. "I don't want to wear those, either."

"But why not? I've never seen them on you."

"No." She was whining now and I wasn't sure I liked it. And I also wasn't sure I liked the idea of giving a child too many choices. So I grabbed the pair of Timberland hiking boots and handed them to her.

"You're wearing these."

She looked up at me. "Okay."

Okay?

After she'd gotten them on and I'd tied them, I stood up and gave her a quick pat on the behind, and when I did her Pull-Up made a crinkling sound under my hand.

"Do you have to pee?" I asked, taking her hand as we left her room and going into the hallway. Lynn had started toilet training her a few months ago, and though there'd been some progress—Nicole tugging on Lynn's arm, telling her she had just peed or pooped, and only once in a great while that she had to go but hadn't yet—it was too intermittent to trust. So Lynn told me I had to ask Nicole as much as I could, even though it annoyed her.

"No."

"Are you sure?"

"Yes."

"You're sure."

"Auntie La*La*. I don't have to pee."

"Well, I do," I said, but we went downstairs anyway.

Lynn and Paul had bought the big old drafty turn-of-the-century stone house almost four years ago, and since then they'd done some structural work on it—installing a new roof and new plumbing and getting all three fireplaces in working order. The bathrooms and the kitchen still needed to be updated, though, but once Nicole was born, they said they didn't have the energy to deal with contractors and architects and builders. They also didn't have the money yet for such renovations. But they'd furnished it nicely with a combination of thrift-store antiques and some new slipcovered couches and chairs that looked like thrift-store antiques, so the overall effect was comfortable. And Pickle-friendly.

Nicole and I arrived in the kitchen to find my mother in complete command. Pots were on the stove and the turkey was splayed, legs in the air, on the counter in a huge roasting pan waiting for its first basting, and she had set my father up with a cutting board and a pile of apples to be peeled and cored and sliced for a pie. Gray-haired and both dressed the same—wearing jeans and sweatshirts and little quilted down vests that left their arms free—they each gave Nicole a big kiss and set about getting her fed.

Or at least talking about getting her fed.

"Do you think she drinks orange juice yet?" my father asked my mother, his hand on the refrigerator door. Before she had a chance to answer, he said, "And cereal? Do you think she eats cereal or"—he opened the refrigerator now and looked inside with obvious confusion—"or eggs? Or oatmeal?" He shut the door and looked helplessly at my mother, who said in rapid staccato succession: "Apple juice. Frozen waffle. She hates eggs, and the only cereal she'd eat is Life, but Lynn's out of it." Then they both fanned out around Nicole to open drawers and cabinets, looking for sippy-cups and plastic plates to put her breakfast on.

In all their efforts, they barely noticed me, which I was secretly glad about, as I was not awake yet and ready for conversation. I poured myself a cup of coffee and sat down at the kitchen table next to Lynn, who was sipping tea from a mug and listening to the whole exchange, dumbfounded that they weren't even bothering to consult her.

"Hi," I said.

"Hi."

"Everything okay?"

"Sure. I mean, I'm just the mother who feeds my child every day, but why should they ask me what she eats? Not to mention the fact that it's *my* Thanksgiving dinner in *my* house, but I didn't really want to have anything to do with it."

"Are you feeling—"

"Infantilized? Yes."

"Do you want to—"

"Say something and start World War III? No. I'll just regress here in silence."

I told Lynn to go up and shower and get dressed and take

her time while I helped feed Nicole. She finished her tea in one big disgruntled gulp and left the kitchen. I took the box of Eggo waffles out of my father's hand and told him I'd take over, so I toasted two waffles—one for Nicole and one for me.

"Auntie LaLa, you have to cut my waffle for me," Nicole said at my side.

"What do you say?"

"Please."

"Please what?"

She giggled. "Auntie LaLa!"

I finished buttering hers and started cutting into it, when she screamed. I dropped the knife, terrified that I'd somehow sliced off her finger.

"I want you to cut it the way Mum-Mum cuts it!"

I looked at her.

"Please."

"Okay. How does Mum-Mum cut it? In half like this?"

She nodded. "But smaller."

"So she cuts it again. Like this?"

She nodded. "But smaller."

I sliced the waffle once more, then handed her the plate of bite-size waffle cubes. I brought my plate over next to hers, then sliced mine in eighths, too.

"You cut your waffle the same as mine, Auntie LaLa."

"I know. I wanted to be just like you."

"We're the same."

"Yup. We're the same."

After we finished eating, we went into the dining room and took the good dishes out of the built-in china cabinets, and I set the table, explaining as I went along about plates and napkins and silverware and tablecloths. Like she cared.

By two in the afternoon, the table was set and the food was just about ready and everyone had dressed for dinner— Nicole in a new green velvet dress with white lace tights and heavy-soled faux Doc Martens ankle boots. She couldn't have looked cuter. She and Lynn and I went into the living room to find Paul, who was on his hands and knees building a fire. If Malcolm had been there, he would have offered to do that task—he took great pride in his ability to build the perfect fire. I wondered where he was then—what he'd decided to do and how he was holding up under the strain of his memories. I thought there might be enough time to call him before dinner, but just as I got the cordless phone and tried to find a quiet place to go, I heard my mother call all of us to dinner.

"Well, this looks great," Paul said as he moved into position at the head of the table. Lynn and my mother and I were bringing things out from the kitchen. Once we'd all sat down, plates started being passed left and right—turkey, stuffing, baked potatoes, asparagus, chopped liver (a new "low fat" recipe from someone my parents had met at one of their Elderhostels)—and Lynn made a plate of food for Nicole.

"No asparagrass, Mum-Mum."

"Okay. You don't have to have any asparagrass."

"And I don't want any sweet potatoes," I chimed in.

Lynn glanced at me over Nicole's hair. "Don't worry. I know all about your fear of orange vegetables."

"It's not my fault," I said, catching my mother's eye. "If someone who shall remain nameless hadn't force-fed me cooked carrots when I was four, I probably wouldn't have an issue with them."

"I didn't force-feed you carrots," my mother said.

"Excuse me, but I seem to remember you prying my mouth open and shoving them in until I gagged." I turned to Nicole and pretended I was barfing. "Carrots are yucky."

She made a face back. "Carrots are yucky," she parroted. I stared at my mother and smiled in victory. How old was I?

A few minutes of silverware clanging and chewing and compliments to the chef ensued before Nicole announced that she could eat her stuffing with her hands.

"Can you eat it with your fork, please?" Lynn said, which made me laugh. I always made fun of how she asked Nicole to do something instead of telling her to do it, and how she always said please, too—as if there were a choice.

Nicole picked up a hunk of stuffing and put it in her mouth with her hand and then giggled. Chunks of breading and celery and onion were all over her face and dropping off in clumps onto her beautiful green velvet dress. Our mother looked on disapprovingly. "Tell her to—"

"Tell her to what?" Lynn snapped.

"To stop—"

"To stop what?"

"She has to learn that she can't—"

"She's only three and a half, okay? Three-and-a-half-year-olds don't understand the concept of 'having to learn that they can't.' "

"She might not understand it, but at least she'll learn that she needs to behave herself during—"

"She doesn't need to behave herself during—"

"It's just us," I said. "It's just—"

"Family," Lynn finished.

"I know it's just family, but even with family, she should learn how to behave."

"Why?" Lynn said, and put her fork down. "Just because we were pathologically well behaved—"

"Like Stepford children," I said.

"Doesn't mean she should be raised like that."

"Raised like what?" my mother asked. She put her fork down and looked umbraged.

"Always afraid of making a mess," Lynn started.

"Or getting yelled at," I added.

"You weren't always getting yelled at."

Lynn shook her head. "Yes, we were."

"No, you weren't."

I shook my head now, too. "Yes, we were."

Paul lifted the plate of white meat turkey and smiled at it. "Does anyone want more?" He had long since appointed himself the family-pathology-ignorer during get-togethers like this, and he was playing his part again now with obvious relish.

"I'll take a little if no one else is going to have any more," my father said, comparing what was on his plate to what was on everyone else's in order to reassure himself that he wasn't a pig. He'd always been somewhat phobic about overeating—especially at holiday meals—which was why, deep into his sixties, he was still so trim.

"It doesn't matter if anyone else is going to have any more or not," Lynn said. "You can have more. You can have more of anything you want. It's a free country."

"Well, I don't want to make a pig of myself." Again he looked around at everyone's plate.

Lynn looked at him in disbelief. "A pig of yourself?" she said. "You eat like a woman."

"A woman on a diet," I said.

She nodded over at me. "He weighs less than me. Not that that's saying much."

"He weighs less than me, too," I echoed, "not that that's saying much, either."

"Well," my mother continued in her tone of high umbrage, "if you think you were always getting yelled at—"

"I didn't say we were always getting yelled at," Lynn clarified. "I said we were always *afraid* of getting yelled at."

"Don't start with me."

"Start what with you?"

"Mincing words."

"I'm not mincing words. Getting yelled at and being afraid of getting yelled at are—"

"Two very different things," I piped in.

"Oh. Another country heard from."

"She's allowed to talk," Lynn said, rushing to my defense.

My mother made her famous face: mouth turned down at the sides, neck muscles taut. Clearly we were headed for disaster. "Okay. I see."

"See what?"

"You're ganging up on me."

"We are not," I said unconvincingly.

"Yes, you are. You're saying 'we.' "

"Now who's mincing words?" Lynn said.

"I think what your mother's trying to say," my father said, "is—"

"I don't need a translator."

"She meant that Nicole should be controlled."

"Disciplined," my mother corrected.

"If you're saying that I should squeeze the life out of her—"

"I'm not saying you should squeeze the—"

"Or that I should break her will until she's completely compliant and—"

"Submissive," I offered. God, would I have to go back to therapy?

"Like we were—then I'm not interested."

"Being told 'no' once in a while isn't the worst thing in the—"

"Having your will broken and your spirit crushed at the age of three and a half isn't exactly what we had in mind."

Paul looked up from his plate, which he'd been concentrating on with false intent in order to avoid entering the fray. "Are you talking to me?"

"I was *say*ing," Lynn said, glaring at him for support, "that breaking Nicole's will and crushing her spirit isn't the kind of parenting philosophy we subscribe to."

"It isn't?"

"No." Lynn threw a pea at him, and then Nicole threw a pea at him.

"Well," he said, picking one pea off his lap and the other out of his hair. "Maybe it should be."

AFTER DINNER WAS over, when Nicole had finally gone down for a nap, taking Paul along with her; after Lynn and I had apologized to my mother for regressing and my parents had gone out for their daily walk despite the cold, Lynn and I went into the back room, which served as a den. She looked exhausted as she cleared a path for herself on the couch and sat down, pushing toys and dolls and stuffed animals out of the way.

"Well, that was a nightmare," she said.

I sighed. "I know. But at least it's over."

"Over? It's only Thursday afternoon. There are three more days left until Sunday."

"That's true, though the big fight is out of the way. Anything now will just feel like little aftershocks."

"You're right," she said, putting her legs up onto the coffee table. "So. How are things?"

I shrugged. "They're okay."

She winced, then lifted herself off the couch.

"Shit!" She pulled out a hard plastic pointy windmill-wand and rolled her eyes. "It's a good thing I'm so fat now, otherwise I would have really felt this."

"You're not fat."

"Yes, I am." She let out her stomach and let her arms and legs go limp so she would look as bloated and bloblike as possible.

"You're *not fat*," I repeated emphatically, thinking we sounded frighteningly like Karen and her sister Gail. "It's just that you used to be really thin, so now you just look normal, like the rest of us."

"Whatever."

We smiled at each other. I loved sitting with Lynn like this. It reminded me of when we were younger and our parents would go out and we'd have the house to ourselves.

"So how are things going with . . . ?"

"Malcolm? They're fine. They're the same."

"So no change."

"Nope."

Though she and I were close and though we were never judgmental with each other, I had learned over the years not to say too much—otherwise she'd worry about me more than she already did.

"What are you going to do?"

"About him? I don't know yet."

"Maybe you should—" She hesitated, I knew, because she didn't want to sound disapproving, or like she was going to tell me what to do. "I mean, since you want kids, maybe he's not the most promising prospect. Not that it's any of my business."

"No, you're right," I said. "I should probably start thinking about finding someone else. Especially since I'm running out of time."

"You're not running out of time. You've got plenty of time. Lots of women don't start having kids until they're forty."

"But I don't want to be forty. I don't want to be that old and doing it for the first time. I barely have enough energy now, for myself."

"I know," she said. "Maybe if I'd had Nicole earlier, I wouldn't be so exhausted all the time."

"Should I"—I blurted out suddenly, then held my breath—"have one? A baby?"

"Of course you should."

Maybe she didn't understand what I meant.

"I mean alone," I clarified.

"Sure."

The simplicity and surety of Lynn's response took me by complete surprise.

"So you don't think it's wrong?"

"Wrong how?"

"You know, like, not good for the child. To have only one parent. Selfish."

"No. It's definitely something to weigh because it's an important issue. But there are far worse things a child could have to deal with than that, I'd say."

"I've been looking into it a little—you know, how I'd do it if I decided to do it. Someday. Do you think I'm crazy?"

"No. I don't think you're crazy. It's just that it's a lot of work, though." She let her head roll back onto the sofa cushion. "A lot of work."

"I know."

"It's hard enough having a child when you're married. But at least there's some help, some relief, at the end of the day, when you think you'll shoot yourself if you're alone with the baby for one more minute." She reflected on it, and even the thought seemed to exhaust her. "I can't really picture that. Doing it by myself."

"I can't, either, really." I shifted uncomfortably on the couch. I couldn't help feeling slightly defensive about having her tell me how hard it would be. As if I hadn't already taken that aspect into consideration.

"I wasn't trying to imply that you were romanticizing having a baby alone."

"Because I'm not."

"I know. It's just that you have to really want a baby. Really, really want one. Having a baby changes everything. Everything. In your entire life. Forever. No one ever tells you that. Or if they do, you don't believe them, or you're not listening."

"Changes it how? You know, besides the obvious ways—no time, no privacy, no selfishness."

"Well, in those obvious ways, like you said. But there are other things that happen—things you don't expect." I waited while she gathered her thoughts. "Like, you lose yourself. You completely lose a sense of who you are. Not that it would matter, since you become a totally different person afterward anyway. But I don't know, it's almost like you forget who you were; forget what it was like to be the way you used to be. Your body changes, your mind changes, your marriage changes, everything changes so suddenly and so completely that it takes a while to realize the extent of what's happened. You get glimpses sometimes, here and there, of how things used to be—late at night when you're too exhausted to go to sleep after a feeding, or at the end of the day when you've just put them down and you have the first moment of peace and quiet that you've had all day—it's like a flashback. You have this vague, distant memory of this person, this life, you used to know—*I used to look like this, and I used to wear this, and I used to think about this and read about that*—only it's gone, and it's been replaced by this other person and this other life. It's not a bad thing. That's not the point. It's just different."

"Do you ever—?"

"Regret it?" She shook her head emphatically. "No. Not at all. Never. I mean, now I can't imagine not having Nicole. I just can't imagine it. I'm only telling you because you should know. You should know before you make any decisions, so that when you decide—if you decide—to do it, you'll be prepared. More prepared than I was."

"Thanks," I said.

"That's what older sisters are for. Advice that sounds condescending but isn't meant to be."

"I didn't think you were being condescending. I just get tired sometimes of people who have kids making it sound like people who don't have kids can't possibly understand what it's like to have them. But to the extent that I can imagine it and based on what I've observed, I think I can make a fairly sound judgment on whether or not I want to get pregnant."

"I'm sure you can. And it sounds like you really want to. I think you want to more than I did before I had Nicole." She refolded her legs underneath her. "And you'd obviously be a great mother, seeing as how you can't get enough of her." She pointed toward the Pickle's bedroom.

I picked up one of Nicole's teddy bears and picked the fuzz off its fur.

"How would you do it?" she started. "Is there someone you could—"

"I have no idea. I've just started thinking about it. I mean, it's not like I'm going to do anything about it tomorrow. I've got too much research to do first."

"I know."

We looked out the window and listened to the wind pushing through the trees. The sky was bright yellow and pink behind the naked branches; the sun would be going down soon. Just then we heard the front door open and close, then my parents talking as they took off their shoes and padded through the kitchen to where we were.

"Hey, Karen's pregnant again," I said, remembering suddenly that I hadn't told any of them.

"So am I," Lynn said.

My eyes went immediately and involuntarily down to her abdomen, looking to see if I'd missed the telltale signs of obvious pregnancy again, as I had with Karen. While my parents squealed with joy and smothered her with hugs and kisses I couldn't help but feel a pang of jealousy swiftly followed by a sense that time was slipping away. I'd always dreamed of Lynn's children and mine growing up together, and if I didn't start soon, too many years would be between them.

"Wow," I said, almost to myself. "That's great. That's amazing. Congratulations."

She smiled and looked happy. Really happy. "We didn't want to say anything until the first trimester was over. Until we were sure it was going to take."

"So the Pickle is going to have a sibling," I said slowly.

"And you're going to have another Pickle," my mother said.

"There's only one Pickle," I corrected, stating the obvious.

"Unless you have your own," Lynn said.

My parents' eyes—gaping, horrified, shocked—nailed me, while Lynn's lips formed the word *oops,* and she covered her mouth with her hands.

"Is there something we should know?" my mother asked.

"Something you want to tell us?" my father added.

"Re*lax,*" I said. "It was just a rhetorical statement. Meaning, like, someday, in the future. I do plan on having a future, you know."

"Of course you have a future," my father said.

"We never said you wouldn't have a future," my mother added.

I shook my head dismissively, but the idea of my having a baby was still shimmering in my mind like a mirage—receding and advancing; real and unreal. I turned back to Lynn, hoping to return the focus to her. "So when are you due?"

"July," she said, smiling.

I COULD BELIEVE anything at this point—including the Pickle's assertion, later that evening when I was putting her

to bed, that the reason she'd peed in her Pull-Up this time
was because she didn't know where the bathroom was.

"You know where the bathroom is."

She shook her head.

"Yes, you do. It's right there." I pointed at her bedroom
door and beyond toward the hallway. "Maybe you should go
now before you go to sleep."

"No way," she said.

"Yes way."

"No way."

"Yes way."

I grabbed both cheeks and got in her face as close as I
could without touching her.

"Nose kiss!" I ordered.

"Nose kiss!" she repeated, and then she grabbed my face,
too, and we rubbed noses and wrestled each other and rolled
around on the bed until I was exhausted.

It was time to go to sleep by then—Nicole's bedtime, not
mine, though I was so exhausted by the end of the day that I
was ready to collapse. I got into bed with her, under the cov-
ers, and read her a pile of books. By the fifth story, our eyes
were drooping, so I finished the one we were in the middle
of, *Blueberries for Sal,* then slid out of bed and turned the
Barney night-light on and the big light off.

I got back in bed and pulled the Winnie-the-Pooh com-
forter up under her neck and breathed deeply. It had been a
long day, a very long day, and my mind was still racing from
my sister's news. Would they have a boy this time, and would
they want to know beforehand, unlike the first time with
Nicole, when they wanted to be surprised? How would
Nicole react to a new little brother or sister, and how would
I react to being an aunt for the second time? Could I ever
feel for the new baby what I'd come to feel for Nicole, or
was she always going to be my favorite? I wondered sud-

denly what she would be like in a few years when she was older. Would she always be as headstrong and opinionated and sure of herself as she was now? Would she keep painting and become an artist, or would a sudden fascination with Lego building blocks emerge and make her want to become an architect or a mathematician? Would we always be as close as we were now? Would she still like me? Or would her growing up inevitably mean our growing apart? And when I leaned over to kiss her, I couldn't help imagining what my child would be like, look like, grow up into, if I had a child.

"Good night, my Pickle."

"Good night," she said. *"I la loo."*

"I la loo, too," I said back.

I went to sleep in tears, so moved by the simple bliss of her declaration that I was unable to think about anything else before I fell asleep—except wanting a child of my own, and what I was going to do to make that happen.

THE

SECOND

TRIMESTER

10

. . .

YOU'D THINK, FROM the way Simon was talking about it, that Karen's baby shower was going to be the event of the season.

"It's going to be the event of the season," he said, the first week of January when we all got back after the Christmas/New Year's break. He licked his lips and I knew he was eager to get back into the swing of things.

Unlike me. I was still staggering through the day, not having fully recovered from spending so much time with my family—first in November and then again in December. But it wasn't just that. A lot had happened during that time: Amy's meltdown and our agreed-on decision deadline; Lynn's announcement that she was pregnant and her essentially giving me permission to have a baby alone; my knowing that a resolution of my relationship with Malcolm was drawing near. It had been a tough few months, and I felt exhausted and emotionally drained.

Simon chased me into my office, shut the door behind him, and lit up a Dunhill. He wasn't allowed to smoke at his desk anymore now that Karen was pregnant, which was too bad since the pressure of the shower arrangements were clearly starting to overwhelm him.

"There's so much to do, you can't imagine."

"It's a baby shower," I said, "not our spring show. What's the big deal?"

He looked at me as if I couldn't be serious.

"You can't be serious. It's for *Karen*." He said her name reverentially, breathlessly, fearfully, as if he were the elected president of the Cult of Karen. "Everything has to be perfect. You know how she gets when it isn't."

I couldn't help but smile. Simon was *so* weird.

"Gail wanted to reserve that muraled room at the Pierre, but Karen said she wouldn't come if we had it there. Too old-ladyish. Then we all agreed on the Royalton—the restaurant and the lobby bar. But when Gail spoke to Martha, she offered to have it at her house in Connecticut, only the date didn't work out."

I was flipping through some message slips and only half-listening, so I looked up to get clarification.

"Martha—?"

"Stewart. She'll mastermind the food and flowers, of course, as well as the overall concept."

Concept? As in, celebration?

"But we're going to have it at Gail's."

"In Oyster Bay?"

"No. At her East Hampton house. It's going to need a complete overhaul for the party, but it'll have to do. Anyway," Simon continued, "Nora's going to word the invitation."

Ephron.

"Celine's promised to sing."

Dion.

"And we've already confirmed a few definites when we were choosing the date: Barbara. Julia. And of course, Demi."

Walters.

Roberts.

Moore.

Karen's A-list clients.

"So what *is* the date?"

"Sunday. May 1. A save-the-date card will go out as soon as we finalize the guest list."

A save-the-date card. Nearly four months ahead of time? Please.

Simon, by now, had pulled a note card out of his suit jacket pocket—presumably a to-do list. I cringed at the thought of getting sucked into the teeth of this thing.

"Annette's overseeing the printing and mailing of the invitations," he began.

And the postmaster general has already started designing a new set of fashion stamps to be issued especially for the occasion. . . .

"Gail and I are doing the first and second drafts of the guest list, which we'll need you to look over and finalize."

And then encrypt in a code that only our three secret decoder rings will be able to crack. . . .

"And Renee is in charge of the cake."

Now that was a deeply ironic idea. I wondered if that meant seven naked men would come gyrating out of it in leather diapers, ready to be changed.

"And you," he said, because of course we hadn't given me my little job yet, "you're in charge of the gift."

"The gift?"

"From the staff. You know, 'With love and obsequiousness from all your loyal worker bees.' That sort of thing."

"*Slaves* would be more appropriate."

He waved me away. Clearly he didn't have time for semantics right now.

When he and his ridiculous list finally left my office, I sat on the edge of my desk and wondered how I was going to summon the energy to participate in yet another baby shower—

especially one that promised to be as high profile and full of ridiculously ostentatious gift-giving as this. I was also worried: What do you get for the Vulcan who has everything?

NOT THAT I would have admitted it to Simon, but I was too distracted to become as obsessed about Karen's gift as he was.

Since Thanksgiving, Amy and I had been spending most of our free time immersed in reading material—the first step, I always believed, in laying the proper foundation for making any decision—but especially a decision as hugely important and irreversible as having a baby. The pile on my desk at home and the other on the table by my bed was growing week after week, month after month—an irony I couldn't help but appreciate—and on the nights and weekends I didn't stay over at Malcolm's, I would read a few general, theoretical, overview-type chapters from Penelope Leach's oeuvre or Dr. Spock's oeuvre or T. Berry Brazelton's oeuvre before I fell asleep.

For my practical reading, I figured I'd start with the easiest book first—*The Girlfriend's Guide to Pregnancy*—then work myself up to the *What to Expect When You're Expecting* three-volume Proust-length trilogy. The *Girlfriend's Guide* was self-described on its back cover in bright pink type as the book that tells you "what to expect when going from *being* a babe to *having* one" (my italics).

I eyed the roll of stomach flab on which the book was resting.

Well, at least in my case, the transformation from before to after wouldn't be so dramatic.

I flipped through the pages and right off the bat eliminated the need to carefully read about half the book since it was chock-full of such useless sections as these:

"Telling Your Husband You're Pregnant."

"Husbands as Birth Coaches."

"Husbands and Your Body Changes."

"Husbands' Fears."

"Husbands' Involvement in Pregnancy."

"Husbands' Involvement in Labor and Delivery."

"Husbands and Massages."

"Husbands and Pregnant Sex." (Please.)

I stapled those chapters shut so I wouldn't have to keep looking at them and being constantly reminded of the annoying fact that husbands usually were part of a woman's pregnancy, even if they weren't going to be part of mine.

If even *I* were going to be a part of mine.

Then I read on.

"Stretch Marks."

"Hemorrhoids."

"Accelerated Nail Growth."

"Accelerated Hair Growth" (which I made a note to tell Amy about so she could kill two birds with one stone by getting pregnant *and* filling in that bald spot).

"Digestion."

"Dementia."

At this point, I decided to limit the subject matter of my reading to the first trimester of pregnancy—keeping things linear and thereby not getting too far ahead of myself. After all, it seemed pointless to worry now about episiotomies, loss of bladder control, cesarean scars, edema, varicose veins, amniocentesis, fetoscopy, and chorionic villus sampling. I could save those for later and *really* have something to look forward to.

Morning sickness was one of the hallmarks of the first three months of pregnancy, so it seemed obvious that I should familiarize myself with the subject, even though I'd had just about enough of it after reading Arlene Schiffler's previous month's stupid diary entry. And when I finished with the *Girlfriend's* "Ten Commandments of Morning Sickness," I went on to *What to Expect When You're*

Expecting. I got a pad of paper ready and kept it handy in case inspiration struck and I wanted to make a list, or a flow chart, or just scrawl a lot of annoyed sarcastic comments in the margins.

On first flip, I was off to a bad start again. A gazillion references to husbands and fathers-to-be littered the pages and put me off until I read a brief section at the beginning of the book with the header, "Being a Single Mother."

> Something you might want to keep in mind when reading this book: the many references to "husband" and "father to be" aren't meant to exclude you. Since the majority of our readers are in traditional families, it's just simpler to use these terms consistently than try to include all the other possibilities that exist.

I see.

So no traditional nontraditional terms like:

Sperm donor.

Or *biological father.*

Or *nonparental biological father.*

Or *nonfamilial birth partner.*

Or *accidental pregnancy fantasy disorder sperm-harvest victim.*

Hankering for alternative nomenclature, I turned to the Internet. But when an initial search turned up a potpourri of available services that were a little too nontraditional for me—including a matchmaking service for complete strangers who wanted to find someone—anyone—with whom to "coparent" a child—I decided to go back to my books. Blacking out the word *husband* or stapling a few pages here and there seemed almost normal by comparison.

"WHAT DO YOU think about adoption?" Amy asked one freezing-cold Sunday afternoon in mid-January, when we came back to my apartment from a fruitless preliminary shopping trip for Karen's present.

"Adoption?" I blew on the tips of my fingers while water boiled in the kitchen for hot chocolate. "Adoption is fine. If you can't have your own. But I want my own."

"But what if you couldn't?"

"Couldn't what?"

"Have your own."

"Then I would adopt."

Maybe.

Better find a good book on that, too.

She flipped through *Beyond Jennifer and Jason: An Enlightened Guide to Naming Your Baby*—a book that contained every pretentious name in the universe and told which celebrity-children had them—but was clearly not reading it.

"I'll probably end up adopting."

"Why?"

"Because I'm convinced I'm sterile."

"*Sterile?*" I repeated in the most dramatic tone I could manage. "What kind of word is that? *Infertile,* maybe. *Fertility-challenged,* even. But not *sterile.*" I went into the kitchen and came back out with two big cups of hot cocoa, then sat down next to Amy on the couch. We were going to need chocolate to get through this conversation. "What makes you even *say* that?"

"I don't know. I've just always suspected that I was."

"But why? Do you have any rational basis for thinking that?"

She shrugged.

"Some loser doctor at Planned Parenthood tell you that ten years ago when he misdiagnosed a yeast infection as syphilis?"

"No." She put the name book down and picked up her cup. "It's just that I've never been pregnant."

"Well, neither have I." I was getting more confused by the minute. "Isn't that why we've embarked on our Decision Journey? To decide whether or not we *should* be someday?"

"Yeah, but . . ."

"But what?"

She paused. "It's just that sometimes I've gone without birth control and nothing's happened."

"You mean, over the course of your lifetime?"

She didn't answer.

"When are you talking about?"

She eyed me through the steam rising from her cup.

"Are you talking about with Will?" I asked. "With Will *now*?"

She nodded.

"What do you mean, you've gone without birth control with Will?"

"I kind of stopped using it."

"Since when?"

"The past month and a half. Since Thanksgiving."

I sat back on the couch.

"Does he know?" I asked.

"No."

"You haven't told him."

"No."

I tried to read her face. "You're still doing it."

She nodded.

"So you've been playing a secret game of Russian roulette and waiting to see if you hit." I felt a wave of concern hit the pit of my stomach, and I sat forward on the edge of the couch waiting for her to explain herself.

But she didn't.

"I don't understand why you're doing this," I said. "Why you're being so cavalier about something so potentially life-altering."

Her whole body shrugged.

"I'm tired of waiting—waiting for Will to do something, waiting for something to fall from the sky that will shake things up and push me in a different direction. I'm a fucking lawyer. I take action and make big decisions every day. I don't see why I can't do the same in my personal life."

"But you haven't thought this through yet. You haven't figured out how you'd do it."

"Yes, I have," she said defiantly. "Just the way I was doing it. Accidentally. It's better than a sperm bank."

"I didn't mean how you'd get pregnant. I mean *logistics*. How you'd manage. You know, money. Child care. Job. Like, are you going to get a nanny and keep working? Or would you want to work only part time? Could you afford to cut back your hours to be home more, and would your firm even allow it?" I felt like I was talking to a ten-year-old.

"Lots of single women have gotten pregnant accidentally and managed, and they've made much less money than I do."

"I'm not just talking about money. Or managing. Or just getting by. I'm talking about being prepared. It's a whole different thing if you're doing it alone. It takes a lot of planning and rational thought if you're going to do it alone, and feel good about doing it alone. And what about Will?"

"What *about* Will?"

"Well, don't you think there's a moral dilemma here? Getting pregnant accidentally on purpose? Do you think it's fair?"

"Do you think it's fair that he's stringing me along and wasting my prime fertile *childbearing* years?"

Okay. I could see I was going to have to try a different tack here. Up until now, I'd thought I knew what made Amy tick, but suddenly I wasn't so sure.

"What do you think he'd do if it actually happened?" I asked. She played with the handle of her cup. "I don't know."

"Do you think he'd want it? Do you think," I said, pressing her, "that it would force the issue—that it would make him want to get married?"

"I don't know. Maybe."

"*Maybe?* The guy is a perpetual student, and you think he's going to mature overnight and transform himself into the perfect responsible father and husband?"

"Maybe he would. Maybe if he had to, he'd grow up."

"I think you're kidding yourself." An understatement.

"I'm not saying it's probable that he would," she said. "I'm just saying that it's possible."

Probable v. Possible. Lawyers had such a way with words. "Those don't sound like great odds to me."

"Or to me either. But they're better than nothing."

I felt my brow crease as I tried—and failed—to follow her logic. "Why are they better than nothing?"

"Because. Because at least I'd be pregnant. Then one half of the equation would be solved. The rest I could figure out after that."

By the time she left later that evening, I felt I'd managed to talk her out of her reckless dementia and had at least achieved containment on the Accidental-Pregnancy-Fantasy-via-Birth-Control-Boycott-Disorder front.

It hadn't been easy.

Her dogged determination to force a resolution—a change—in the status of her relationship with Will seemed desperate and bizarre, especially since she was the one who had seemed less enamored of the idea of having a baby by herself than I had when we'd first talked about it.

Which was probably what would end up happening if her birth control boycott continued much longer.

And yet, the more I thought about it, the more I realized that that was the point: She *wasn't* planning on having a baby alone.

She was, as she'd admitted earlier, hoping he would hear the news and rally to the challenge—hoping he'd realize, finally, how tired he was of being a retarded and infantile almost-forty-year-old and how this was the perfect way to turn his life around.

And the more I thought about it, the more I realized this was another variation of Amy's disregard for relationship reality—in essence, she'd done the same thing with Jonathan: she'd decided what she wanted, and she would ignore any and all signs that what she wanted was not possible. Only this time the stakes were much higher.

Sadly, I understood her dementia and the fantasy that lay behind it. If Malcolm and I had had sex, I'm sure I would have been thinking the same thoughts and hiding my birth control pills under the mattress, the way crazy patients in mental hospitals always did in the movies.

But I liked to think I was different from Amy.

That I was more rational.

I liked to think that I was in complete control of myself and of my own raging Pregnancy Fantasy Disorder.

"DID YOU KNOW that paraplegics—even quadriplegics— can get their wives pregnant even though they can't, obviously, move around and have sex?" I asked Malcolm later that night.

I'd gone over to his place after Amy had left, and by the time I'd arrived and we'd had our requisite three-hour conversation—this time about the world's growing obsession with gigantic muffins—and were finally getting into bed, it was after two.

"Where'd you read that?"

"I can't remember," I said quickly, even though it was actually true. I just didn't want to admit that what I couldn't remember was which of the three million pregnancy books I had read it in.

He pushed his fist into his pillow. "No. I didn't know that."

"It's because, well, it's because they still have involuntary spasms," I continued, as if he'd asked me to.

" 'Spasms'?"

I nodded.

"Erections," he said. "Let's call a spade a spade."

"Okay. Erections," I repeated. "While the paralysis affects nerves and limbs, it doesn't affect the muscles of the—"

"Penis."

I nodded. "But even if there weren't these involuntary spasms—" I continued.

"Erections."

"Erections—the doctors would still be able to harvest sperm from them clinically. And then impregnate their wives through artificial insemination."

He started to set the alarm clock but stopped.

"Is somebody you know at work married to a paraplegic or a quadriplegic?" he asked.

I shrugged. "No."

"Has Karen suddenly decided to design a line of clothes for people in wheelchairs?"

"No."

"Are you thinking of leaving the fashion industry to become a spinal-cord-injury lobbyist?"

I rolled my eyes. "No."

"Then why are we talking about this?"

Wasn't it completely obvious?

If a woman could get pregnant by a paralyzed man, then I could get pregnant by a—well, by Malcolm.

In control of my own raging Pregnancy Fantasy Disorder. Hardly.

AFTER MALCOLM FELL asleep, I sat up in bed, thinking.

It wasn't just the money.

Or the nanny.

Or the job issues.

And it wasn't just the mystery sperm donor.

Or the ethics of certain psychological impairment to the child as a result of being the product of anonymous artificial insemination.

There was another obstacle getting in the way of my own moving into the how stage—an obstacle that had nothing to do with finances and moral imperatives or the unfathomability of a nameless, faceless "father" whom I still could not imagine—if that was the route I was going to take—if I was going to take any route at all. And it was one that defied logical solutions and practical decisions.

It was the idea of giving up: giving up the possibility, the chance, the hope that it could all still happen in a natural way, in a normal way; that I could still fall in love with someone who wasn't married or who wasn't frozen. Someone who wanted a relationship and could sustain a relationship and didn't have to be begged and prodded and cajoled every step of the way. Someone, in short, who wasn't ambivalent.

This was the line in the sand that separated stage-one thinking from stage-two thinking and beyond—the line that I could not seem to cross.

To give up that chance—to make a decision that would, in fact, remove chance from the equation—seemed monumental, as if I would also have to acknowledge at the same time the removal of a whole host of other possibilities from life as well:

Mystery.

Hope.

Luck.

Romance.

Love.

It was—or seemed to be—the sort of decision a person

without faith makes, a person without a firm belief that their own future will turn out well. And while I had never had much faith in myself, I did have a tiny bit—the bare minimum—enough to make me hesitant about handing it over. And that hesitation left me at a standstill.

Yet time was running out.

It was mid-January, and I was no closer to coming to a decision than I had been three months ago when I'd first started giving the question serious thought.

"THE TWO OF you need to get a fucking life," Renee said the next morning at work. We were, as usual, standing in the kitchen and waiting for the coffee to finish dripping. "I mean, do you and Amy ever talk about anything else besides having kids?"

"No."

"Sounds like a pretty limited friendship to me." She looked smug and self-satisfied. "Unlike our friendship."

"Which is so multilayered, since all we ever do is talk about work." I squeezed a line of dishwashing liquid into my dirty cup and turned the hot water on full blast.

"We talk about other things besides work."

"We do?" I said. "Like what?"

"Like—" she started, then stopped to think. "Like about Amy's loser boyfriend and about my complete lack of boyfriends and about your impoholic boyfriend." She invoked her nickname for Malcolm, which she'd shortened from the long version—the Impotent Alcoholic—and which she used with frequent disdain in order to make it clear that she thought I could do way better than him.

"He's a recovering impohol—I mean, *alcoholic,*" I started. "And he's not impotent. He's—"

"Frozen. Right. I know. You've told me that a thousand times, and I still have no idea what the difference is."

"There's a difference. Trust me."

"Why should I?"

"Because I'm asking you to."

I reached around her hair for a paper towel. "Like our conversations are so varied."

"They are varied. Sometimes I yell at you for being obsessed with getting pregnant. Then I yell at you for being obsessed with getting pregnant and not getting pregnant. I mean, if you want to do it so much, why don't you just fucking do it already?"

"I'm thinking about it."

"You're thinking about it." She looked completely unimpressed. "And what exactly have you been thinking?"

We poured our coffee, and Renee followed me back to my office. I closed my door, and we sat down at my desk, facing each other.

"I've been thinking about doing it," I said, then told her about the nine-month time line.

"And?"

"And what?"

"*And?* What have you decided?"

"I haven't decided anything yet. That's the point of *investigating* something *first,*" I said. "It gives you time to not decide before you decide."

"What's there to think about?" she said, her voice rising. "You know you want a kid. You know you don't want to wait until you're forty. You're going to prolong this whole thing even longer with all your fucking peregrinations. Knowing you, at the end of the nine months, you'll decide you need to think about it for *another* nine months—and then *another* nine months—and before you know it, you'll be forty and you won't want to do it, or you won't have any viable eggs left."

"Look, if reality weren't a consideration, I'd be past the should-I-or-shouldn't-I part and on to the next stage."

"Which is what?"

"Which is how. How, out of all the unnatural clinical futuristic scientific petri-dish ways to get pregnant, I would do it."

"Another reason for you to get rid of that impoholic of yours. So you could possibly get pregnant in a more normal way, like by—"

"Having sex."

"My point exactly."

"That's another conversation."

"That's another twenty conversations."

"Whatever."

She snorted.

I snorted back.

"Well, to me, the reality question isn't so complicated," she said.

"Of course it's complicated. There's money. There's short-term planning and long-term planning. All that stuff."

Another ten-year-old, this one. She and Amy could form their own life-without-practical-considerations-and-conse-quences play group without me. I was pragmatic and pes-simistic to a fault. I'd learned that from my parents.

"Please. You make plenty of money."

"But I'd need more money—a lot more—if I had a kid. Clothes and equipment and a bigger place and child care, since I'd have to keep working to pay for it all. Not to men-tion the cost of artificial insemination itself, if that's what I end up doing. There's a lot that would have to be figured out."

"Okay, fine. So you figure out the money. What else?"

"Well, there's the whole ethical question. You know, is it right to choose to have a child alone? Is it selfish to condemn a child to having only one parent? To having no father? And if you have a sperm-bank baby, what do you tell it when it gets old enough to want to know who its other parent is? How do you justify the fact that the child will never ever know who the father was, what he looked like, what he sounded or talked like—that there will always be this incomprehensibly huge blank—this missing piece—at the core of its being?" I took a breath and went on. "I mean, there's no research on this yet," I continued. "A whole generation of sperm-bank babies hasn't grown up yet. Who knows what new strains of psychological damage will emerge from this?"

Renee thought a minute before shrugging off my misgivings.

"There are worse things a kid can have to deal with," she said.

"Oh, really," I said. "Like what, Dr. Spock?"

"Like abusive parents. Child-beating parents. Alcoholic parents."

"Infanticidal parents," I added sarcastically. "Münchhausen-by-proxy parents. You're talking about extremes."

"Okay. Then parents who fight all the time and who make their kids' lives miserable, like mine did, so that they grow up and never want to get married and never want to have kids because they wouldn't want their kids to be as miserable as they were."

"Maybe," I said. Renee frequently alluded to her own particularly unhappy childhood, only the bare bones of which I knew: an Upper West Side childhood, punctuated by a messy prolonged divorce when she was twelve. Magazine editor father remarries and moves to Princeton,

New Jersey, where he starts a new family by having two more children. Renee, her brother Randy, and high-school teacher mother fall on hard times due to their father's lack of child support payments and move downtown. "End of story," Renee would always say at that point, so that was all I knew.

"Or absentee parents, like Karen," she added.

Okay.

True.

"They should have just taken Marissa straight out of the delivery room and put her into therapy so she could get started already, she's going to be so unbelievably fucked up." She lit a cigarette and threw the match into my wastebasket.

I watched her blow smoke rings in silence.

"All I'm saying, Ellen, is that if you want something badly enough, you do it, and you let everything else figure itself out. Otherwise you'll do nothing. And you'll have nothing." She stood up and started for the door, but then turned back to me. "And then I'll *really* be stuck with you."

11

. . .

THERE WERE ONLY eighty-eight shopping days left before Karen's shower.

Then eighty-seven.

Then eighty-six.

Then eighty-five.

I knew this constant countdown because Simon E-mailed me every day to ensure I had a gift—the perfect gift—ready and wrapped—by May 1.

```
Eighty-eight days left.
Something deft,
perhaps, to hide her postnatal heft?
```

Or:

```
Eighty-six.
Make your picks
While the clock still ticks.
```

Until I wrote back:

Eighty-four.
Eighty-three.
Eighty-two.
Eighty-one.
E-mail me again
And I'll get a gun.

It was, however, as Martha Stewart herself would say, "a good thing" that Simon was annoying me every day with his E-mails, otherwise I might never have started looking in earnest, albeit reluctantly, for the baby gift of the century.

After his tenth E-mail, I asked Jennifer to bring in whatever catalogs we received and shelved at the office—Tiffany, Bergdorf Goodman, Saks Fifth Avenue—as well as the other mail-order catalogs that carried everything from bedding and maternity clothes and baby clothes to strollers and cribs and toys. Yet after studying them at my desk one afternoon in early February and not seeing anything that was even remotely suitable for Karen, I realized that the only person who would really know what you were supposed to give someone like Karen was Karen.

Or someone in Karen's fame-and-financial bracket.

To wit, I asked Jennifer to start calling our famous clients' assistants to find out what their bosses had been given when they'd had their kids. Two days later we went over the results of her telephone survey together in my office.

I sat back in my chair and gummed the end of my pen.

"So what did Jodie get from her friends when she had Charles?" I asked, figuring I'd start with the Pregnancies of Unknown Origins first.

Jennifer scanned her pad. She looked like a miniature Karen with her fudge-colored bob and her drapey black KLNY separates and that look in her eye—hunger. Sometimes I even thought I'd caught her hiding her ass as she walked through the office, but I was probably just imagining it. She was young and full of ambition, and for her Karen was the ultimate success story. Jennifer idolized her, wanted to be her, and really believed—on some level, I was certain—that she could be her. When I'd interviewed her for the job a year ago and asked her where she saw herself in five years (stupid question, I know, but I couldn't resist), she said this: "Being Karen." I'd had to stop myself from laughing out loud at the egregious entitlement in her voice—from leaning across my desk and cackling that she'd be lucky to still have a job in the business in five years. That people like Karen didn't become what they were by accident, or by some errant stroke of luck. They became who they were because they had some spark of genius that shot them up into the universe and separated them from the masses down below. Jennifer didn't have that spark, and neither, I'd realized long ago, did I. And while I had never seen myself as "being Karen," I had longed desperately to be something more than I was; to do something more than I was doing today, trying to track down what baby gifts famous women had gotten from their famous friends.

"Jodie Foster got . . . flowers, and . . . lots of baby clothes," Jennifer reported. "Some really cute things, her assistant said, from agnès b."

"What about Rosie O'Donnell?" I asked, moving into the Single Women Who Adopt category.

"Rosie got . . . the same, basically. Baby clothes, mostly."

"And Michelle Pfeiffer?" I asked, sticking to adoptive mothers.

"Again, baby clothes. Petit Bateau. Dries Van Noten. Paul Smith. And she also got a lot of skin care items."

"Skin care items? For her?" She didn't even give birth, not that that would have had anything to do with a need for skin care items.

"No, for her daughter."

I was totally confused. "What do you mean? Like foundation and powder and blush?"

Jennifer finally laughed a little, though whenever she did,
I always felt like she was laughing *at* me instead of *with* me,
since I suspected she thought I was odd in the same ways
Karen thought I was odd.

"No. Not makeup. *Skin* stuff. From Kiehl's. Crabtree &
Evelyn. And Bulgari."

"Shut *up*," I said. "Bulgari makes *baby lotion?*"

"That's what Diego said." She checked her pad once
more just to be sure.

I shook my head in disgust and told Jennifer she could
leave, and should leave—as in *go home*—since it was well
after seven o'clock by then. Except for a few of the most tor-
tured assistants, almost everyone had left—an early night,
actually, by KLNY standards.

Once she'd gone, I looked out the window at the cold
dark winter sky. Malcolm was teaching and wouldn't be
home till late anyway, so I turned off my office lights and sat
down at the computer.

I figured I would surf around on the Internet to see if I
could get some new brilliant idea about a gift for Karen, but
when the keywords *rocking horse* and *beanbag chairs* yielded
nothing interesting, I tried *piggy banks* and then *stuffed animals.*

I started scrolling down the screen.

```
Animals: Veterinary Medicine:
Veterinarians and Clinics
*Northwest Valley Veterinary Hospital and
Canine Semen Bank—A to Z about services and
canine artificial insemination.
```

Why all the veterinary references? I wondered, before
scrolling up and realizing that I'd forgotten to modify

animals with *stuffed*. I scrolled back down and continued reading:

```
Health: Reproductive Health: Infertility
*Cryos International Sperm Bank Ltd.—special-
izing in the worldwide delivery of high qual-
ity tested donor semen.

Health: Reproduction: Infertility:
Clinics and Practices
*UCSF IVF Program—Provides infertility ser-
vices, including IVF, GIFT, ZIFT, ovum donor,
ICSI, embryo and semen cryo-preservation,
donor sperm bank, and male infertility (in
California).
```

My palms started to itch as my hands hovered about the keyboard, waiting to hit the scroll button every time I read a line of text. I swallowed and blinked, amazed and thrilled and, to be frank, a little horrified, by what I'd just stumbled onto.

```
Health: Cultures and Groups: Lesbian, Gay and
Bisexual:
*Rainbow Flag Health Services—donor sperm bank
serving the gay and lesbian community.

Health: Care Providers: Clinics and Practices:
Reproductive
*Repository—sperm bank. Long-term storage for
frozen sperm and embryos.
```

Host uterus.
Ovary freezing.
Egg banking.
Frozen embryo transfer cycles.

Cryo-preservation.

MicroSort sperm separation.

I mean, I knew you could shop for things on the Internet, but I'd never imagined shopping in cyberspace for space-age cryogenics services.

I went back a few screens and then clicked on *Cryogenesis.* I scanned their main menu, then clicked on *Selecting a sperm donor.* One of the options was *View a Sample Donor Profile.*

A Sample Donor Profile?

I couldn't click fast enough.

Sperm Donor Profile #1049

General Description

First Name:	Christopher
State:	California
Age:	25
Race:	Caucasian
Maternal Ethnic Ancestry:	German
Paternal Ethnic Ancestry:	German
Height:	6′2″
Weight:	185
Hair Color:	Brown & blond
Hair Texture:	Straight
Eye Color:	Green
Physical Build:	Medium
Complexion:	Light
Tanning Ability:	Tans easily
Predominant Hand:	Right
Teeth:	Excellent
Vision:	20/20
Hearing:	Normal
Distinguishing Characteristics:	Dimples on cheeks. Small cleft chin.

Citizenship: USA
Native Tongue: English
Religion: Christian
Practicing: No
Birth Date: 02/69
Blood Type: O negative
Sexual Orientation: Heterosexual
Marital Status: Single
Smoker: No

Hair *texture?*
Tanning ability?
Predominant *hand?*
I read on.

Education / Intelligence

Education: BS/BA
High School Grade
  Point Average: 3.75
College Grade
  Point Average: 3.5
College Major: PoliSci/Econ
SAT Score: 1355

Bullshit his combined SAT scores were 1355. But then I remembered.

This was only a Sample (read: made-up) Donor Profile.

I went on and read how he described himself:

. . . Secure . . . sensitive . . . innovative . . . creative . . . competitive . . . respectful . . . comedic . . . optimistic . . .

Optimistic? Surely he was from a different gene pool from me. Which was a positive thing.

. . . Future goals: Entertainment lawyer; filmmaker.

Was this a sperm bank or a computer dating service?

Whichever it was, I didn't just want to order this guy's sperm. I wanted to *marry* him.

And then, finally, the pièce de résistance:
The sample donor's photo.
Blond. Green eyes. Square jaw. Aquiline nose.
Okay. So this *was* a dating service. And he was the bait.

BY THE TIME I'd gotten to the sample sperm donor's photo, I didn't know what to do with myself. I didn't feel like going home to my apartment—full as it was of useless and outdated reading material. And I didn't think I could handle seeing Malcolm, since all I'd want to do was tell him about everything I'd found on the Internet, and well, *that* would go over like a lead balloon.

First, I buzzed Renee's office. When she didn't answer, I ran down the hallway and saw her door was closed and that she'd left for the day. So then I called Amy and told her about what I'd printed out.

"Did you know that you can access sperm donor profiles on the Web? All you have to do is enter a credit card to browse the entire data bank of donors, which I didn't do yet, of course. But they had a sample profile. And the donor profiles have pictures! *Pictures!*"

I stood up from my desk and started pacing around my office, the phone cord stretched taut.

"Not that I'm sure I would even do any of this," I continued, "but one of the things that's always made me queasy about sperm banks, among other things, was not knowing what the guy looked like. I just couldn't imagine how you'd have a child, and as it grew up, you'd look at it and think, *Well, that's not my nose.* And *That's not my hair.* And you'd have no idea who the hell's they were."

Amy was quiet.

"I'm sorry. Am I boring you?" I asked sarcastically. I felt like I'd been enthusing into a big black hole.

"No. I was just distracted."

I slumped back into my chair.

"I just stumbled onto the most amazing find in cyber-space—just the shot in the arm we've been waiting for—and you're dis*tracted?*" I paused. "May I ask by what?"

"I just broke up with Will."

I JUMPED IN a taxi and was at her apartment about seven minutes after we'd hung up. Once inside, I sat on her couch, breathless and sweating and with my nose running from the cold.

"Speak," I said.

She shrugged as if nothing seismic had occurred.

"I broke up with him. That's basically the long and short of it."

She certainly was unpredictable. Just when I'd thought everything was under control with the no-birth-control incident, she suddenly breaks up with her boyfriend out of the blue.

"I know. You said that already. But why tonight? What happened?"

"I've been thinking about it for a while, you know. I told you that. And then tonight we had a drink, and he told me he wants to take a year off from writing his thesis and from me to go to Wyoming where a friend of his lives and think about everything, and well, I lost it." She shook her head in disgust and disbelief. "I mean, Jesus, taking a year off from doing nothing. How unbelievable is that?"

Pretty unbelievable.

I'd agreed with Malcolm that her relationship with Will wasn't going to work out, but I'd never thought it would unravel like this—him literally getting more "space," and her being brave enough to end it before it devolved any further.

"So how do you feel?"

"Feel?" She repeated the word as if she had no idea what it meant. "I don't really *feel* anything right now. I'm just numb. And beaten. And completely demoralized. To have someone be so ambivalent about you that he has to get away for a year to think about whether he wants to be with you— it's like—please. I've had it. I think I've finally had it." She fell momentarily speechless. "I'm not doing this again."

"Doing what again?"

"Getting involved with a guy who has so many issues about being a couple. Next time—if there is a next time, which, at this point, I doubt there ever will be—I'm going to force myself to find someone less complicated. They might not be as interesting and I might not be as interested in them, but fuck interesting. At least it won't be a total waste of time, like this was."

She started to cry then, and I felt helpless, not knowing what I could say to make her feel better and not wanting to say anything that could possibly make her feel worse.

"Do you think there's a chance he'll—"

"A chance he'll change? That he'll call me tomorrow, or next week, or the week after, and tell me how stupid he was to let me go and how he can't live without me and that he'll beg me to take him back?" Tears streamed down her face, and she tried to wipe them away with the palms of her hands. "No. I wish he would. I'd give anything for him to do that. But I know he won't. He's not ready for any of this. I don't know when he'll be ready, but I know it won't be any-time soon. And I can't wait that long."

1 2

. . .

IN THE WEEKS following Amy's breakup with Will, she'd been resolute in her efforts not to sit around waiting for him to come crawling back.

She was dating.

"Dating, dating, dating," she would say. "I'm a dating machine. Blind dates. Lunch dates. Dinner dates. Drinks. You name it. I'm dating it."

She certainly was.

Dentists.

Periodontists.

Orthodontists.

Podiatrists.

Real estate lawyers.

Real estate developers.

Developmental psychologists.

Psychopharmacologists.

I tried to be enthusiastic and encouraging about every fix-up ("Yes, I'd agree: Bald is a relative term"; "If he's six foot nine, there's a good chance your kids wouldn't be freak-

ishly tall"; "No! I *love* men with red hair!"), since getting out
was better for her than staying in a relationship that was
going nowhere. Just listening to the energy she was expend-
ing on each of these dates exhausted me. And I couldn't help
feeling slightly depressed by her fervor—by her desperation,
it even seemed sometimes—to meet someone—*anyone*—
before it was too late.

"Too late for what?" I'd ask when I was feeling particularly contrary. I thought that playing devil's advocate
might disabuse me of the same time-motivated panic to
become coupled as soon as possible. But Amy would just
look at me and make a face, and I knew that she knew I was
fighting the same race against the clock.

I'd been thinking a lot about my own relationship with
Malcolm ever since I'd printed out the information from the
Internet on sperm banks. Knowing how accessible becoming pregnant could be—how possible it could be—had
made me restless and even a bit bold. I knew I had to make a
change, but I didn't want to settle. I didn't want to give up
someone I loved for someone I might not love as much. Or
at all.

The truth is, I wanted to ask Malcolm to help me have a
baby—surreal, I know, given the context of our relationship.
Still, even though he couldn't sleep with me, and even
though he'd been very clear about not wanting to have any
more children, and even though he hadn't ever told me, I
believed he loved me. And I knew I loved him.

"OF COURSE YOU should ask him," Renee said Sunday
afternoon, when I called her at home to see what she
thought. It was the tail end of March and unusually warm
that day. I'd opened all the windows in my apartment, then
pulled a chair over to the living-room windows and brought

the cordless phone with me. As we talked, I put my bare feet up on the sill and closed my eyes and listened to the noise, unmuffled, unblocked by the double-paned glass, drifting up from the street.

Renee and I rarely talked on the phone at home—partly because we saw each other every day all day, which precluded the need to carry over conversations outside the office, and partly too, I think, because she and I had somehow tacitly set the limitations of our friendship long ago: work friends were work friends, no more, no less. As personal as we got at the office—and we certainly did get personal—I don't think she ever trusted that our friendship would survive, or be relevant, in the outside world.

But I did. And because Amy was out on yet another date and I needed a reality check of major proportions now—I was considering asking someone to father my child—I decided suddenly to change the rules.

"You're sure," I said.

"Of course I'm sure."

"Why?"

"Because he's the logical person to ask. And at the moment, he's the only person to ask. Last time I checked, he was the only impoholic in the picture. Am I wrong?"

"No. You're not wrong. You're never wrong, Renee."

"Well, anyway, he *is* the man you're involved with. The man you're closest to."

"The man I'm in love with."

She went still, completely still, for a moment, then continued on. "The man you're in love with. Think of it this way: He'd probably be insulted if you *didn't* ask him. Talk about an affront to a man's manhood."

Now there was a thought. But I couldn't see Malcolm's answer hinging on something as banal as a bruised or a stroked ego.

"I don't know," I said. "I just can't imagine actually asking him. I literally cannot imagine where and when and how I could ever have that conversation with him. Could you? Could you imagine ever having that conversation with someone?"

"No. But then, I don't want kids."

"I know," I said, watching pedestrians dodge traffic as they crossed the street. "But let's say you did. What would you say, and where would you say it?"

"You could do it in a restaurant. 'Listen, I'm glad you ordered the steak because you're going to need your strength now that I'm going to make you start fucking me.'"

"Oh, God."

"Or you could always do it in bed. 'No, we don't actually have to have *inter*course for me to get pregnant. There are experts and fertility clinics that help impoholics who can't—' "

"Stop it."

"Well, you asked me."

"And I can see now I shouldn't have."

"So what's the alternative?"

"I could have asked Amy." And I would. Tomorrow.

"No, I mean what's the alternative to your question? Not asking? Not asking and never knowing if he'd do it or not because asking is too awkward?"

I thought about it and closed my eyes. Awkwardness seemed a small price to pay for something this important.

"So . . . how . . . what—where—when?" I stammered.

"Well, I think you just have to come out and say it as directly as possible. That this is something you really want to do. That it's something that's incredibly important to you, and that because it's so impotent—I mean im*port*ant—you can't imagine doing it accidentally, or with just anyone, or with someone completely unknown and anonymous. And then you have to do the big disclaimer thing: you know, that you're not looking for any involvement from him—emotionally or financially. That you're completely prepared to do this alone, except for the fertilization part. And that basically that's all you're asking him for."

"Jesus, that's cold," I said. "I mean, that's a pretty unbelievable thing to say to someone. To ask someone, especially someone you're involved with, 'Just give me a baby, and then we don't ever have to have anything to do with each other again.' "

"But that's kind of the point. It's a bargain—a bargain in which he finally has the chance to give you what you want—to give you what you want most in the world—and to feel generous and magnanimous and selfless in the process. Your end of the bargain is to make it as easy as possible for him to do that."

Renee—ever the pragmatist, the cynic. A deal was a deal was a deal: nothing more, nothing less. Here was cynicism in its purest form—striking a deal to create a life. But who's to say she was completely wrong?

"You'd be letting him off the hook," she continued. "You'd be exempting him from obligation. And from what you've told me about how he doesn't want any more kids, that might be the only way he'd ever say yes."

1 3

. . .

"YOU'RE *LETTING ME off the hook?* You're *exempting me from obligation?* Do you know what it means to say what you've just said? Do you have any idea of the implications of those statements? Of what it says about who you think I am to even think I'd agree to something like that?"

Malcolm threw a twenty-dollar bill on the bar at the Cedar Tavern and stormed off through the door outside. The previous night's conversation with Renee had made me brave enough to bring it up, and what had started out as my backing into the subject too quickly when I thought I saw an opening—Malcolm had mentioned an article about fertility doctors he'd just read in *New York* magazine by a writer he knew—had turned into my actually asking the whole question. His rage was far beyond anything I could have imagined.

I picked up my bag and stood up, feeling my legs weaken as I followed him outside. I had never seen him this furious, and I had no idea what to do or say to calm him down.

He was standing on the sidewalk as I came out; his eyes fierce, his face flushed, his hands in fists at his sides.

We weren't through yet.

"I'm sorry," I started. "I'm sorry I asked you. I had no idea you'd react this way." I felt the panic rising in my voice, and I realized I had not prepared myself for a scene like this. "I never meant to insult you, or to imply that—I just assumed that what you'd always said about not wanting to have any more kids was absolute. I thought the only way you might consider doing this was if you didn't have to be a part of it."

"Well, you thought wrong. You don't even know what you asked me, do you? What the exact meaning of your question was." I felt like he hated me suddenly. "Come on, you're the marketing expert who has a facility with words. What exactly did you ask me to do?"

"I asked you—I asked you to help me."

"To help you what?"

"To help me have a child."

"And what else? What else did you ask me for?"

I was so upset, I could hardly think straight.

"Nothing. I didn't ask you for anything else."

"Exactly." He glared at me. "Think about that. And ask yourself what connection that might have to my reaction." He turned, then, and started to walk away.

I stood there trying to take in what he had just said.

"I didn't ask you for anything else because I didn't think you'd want to give me anything else," I yelled at his back.

He stopped and turned.

"I knew that you didn't want the emotional responsibility of children again—of a family again. It's something you've told me over and over, and it's something I'd finally accepted." I lowered my voice and tried to choose my words carefully. "So I thought, this way you wouldn't have to have any responsibility. You wouldn't have to have anything to do with the child or with me if you didn't want to, and I would understand that."

"You don't know me at all, then. And you certainly don't know anything about what it means to have a child."

"What are you talking about?" I could feel how tense his body was, how full of anger it was. The more I said, the worse it was getting, and yet there was no going back now. This was the final demarcation line for him and me, I knew, and though we'd reached this line sooner than I'd expected, we were finally up against it.

"If you knew anything about what having a child really means, you would never have asked me that question," he said. "You couldn't have asked me that question. Because to ask it implies that you think I could have a child and then walk away from it—a scenario that is completely inconceivable to me. Not to mention morally reprehensible. I could never do that. Never in a million years."

He shoved his fists into his pockets and shook his head in disbelief. "Having a child is *sacred*. It's the most *sacred* fucking thing you can do in this world. And for you not to know that—for you not to know what it means—what it means to *me*—it's, well . . ." His voice trailed off in disgust. "I don't know. I don't know what we've been doing the past year."

He ran his hands through his hair, and when he collected himself, he looked at me without disdain for the first time since we'd started arguing.

My eyes welled up, and the tears that rolled down my cheeks stung, as if I'd been slapped across the face.

"I'm sorry," he said softly. "I'm sorry I got so angry."

"I'm sorry, too." I wiped the tears unceremoniously from my face and ran the back of my hand across my nose. "I'm sorry I asked you. This was a mistake. A huge mistake, and I'm sorry. I really am."

I was completely devastated by his reaction, and underneath I was beginning to feel the force of my own anger. His unwillingness to even discuss something I wanted suddenly made me interpret his long-standing behavior in a different way: He wasn't frozen. He was withholding. And that insight—whether right or wrong, I didn't care at that moment—made me shake with rage.

"No matter what I would have asked you for, you would have said no. You've always said no."

I could feel more tears coming, and I looked up at the night sky, clear and black and relentlessly deep, so they would go back behind my eyes.

"So don't tell me that you won't do this because I didn't ask you for more than just your sperm." I took a step toward him and pointed my finger as I spoke. "Don't tell me that if I'd asked you to do this with me—to do this together— you'd have said yes. Because if that's the case, then I'll ask you for that." I looked straight at him, daring myself to go on. "I'll ask you right here, right now, to please do this for me— to please do this with me."

Our eyes locked, and for a second or two neither of us flinched. But then he looked away.

"I can't," he finally whispered. "I'm sorry. But I just can't."

So. It was over finally. Completely over. And I felt empty now, and hollow, and implausibly calm.

"We can talk about it more, if you want to," he said. "Tomorrow, or—whenever. I just don't think we should keep at it tonight."

"There's nothing more to talk about," I said.

He looked down and clenched his jaw. "What are you saying?"

"I'm saying that there's nowhere left for this to go. We want different things, you and me. Completely different things. Torturing each other like this seems pointless, don't you think?"

He looked spent. "What do you want from me, Ellen?"

"I want you to *feel* something. To *want* something. To *fight* for something. To fight for *me*. But you don't want this. You don't want me. Every time you see me, every time we're together, I remind you of everything you can't do anymore. Of everything you don't have anymore. Of everything you lost and think you'll never ever recover. I don't bring you any joy. Any pleasure. Any happiness. I haven't brought you any closer to life. And maybe I've even made things worse."

"You didn't make things worse. You made them better. You helped me."

"Did I?" I was incredulous. I felt like he was talking about a different relationship, two different people who weren't us. "I didn't help you. I disappointed you, and you disappointed me. We failed each other. How does that help anyone?"

"We tried, at least."

"You didn't try. Maybe you couldn't, or you weren't ready to, or you just didn't feel enough for me to want to get better. Maybe next time, with someone else, you will. Maybe when you meet someone who means enough to you, you'll fight for her," I said. "You'll fight to keep her from giving up on you."

And then I walked away.

I DON'T REMEMBER anything about the rest of that night, or much about the week afterward, except a profound sadness and sense of loss—loss of hope, loss of possibility, for what our relationship might have been but did not become. I saw that I had expected too much from Malcolm. I'd wanted something from him that I'd known all along he couldn't give, and as Amy had done with Jonathan and then with Will, I had refused to see it and refused to accept it.

I'd wanted to change him, to fix him, to heal him—to

crack him open like a badly healed bone that needed to be reset—and when I couldn't, and when I realized I had not been important enough to him to make him turn away from his grief and start a new life with me, a thickening sense of failure and melancholy set in. We had loved each other, but maybe not enough. Not enough to have given each other what we wanted most.

Once I accepted the fact that Malcolm wouldn't be a part of my life now or in the future, I became more focused. Having a child—or not—would be solely my decision.

14

. . .

THE TWO BIG birthdays were coming up: Lynn's on April 3 and Nicole's on April 5. In order for me to go to Maine with a semiclear conscience and without worrying that Karen would call me on my cell phone about something I hadn't done or something she just thought I hadn't done, I first needed to get through the mountain of work on my desk.

Samples of the fall line had just come in. They were all black, and gray ("the new black"), and brown ("the other new black"). Suit jackets, skirts, pants, sweaters, shorts, socks, underwear, shoes were draped and hanging and laid out on every possible surface in my office.

And I was starting to hear the *they're just clothes* voice.

"It looks like a Loehmann's dressing room in here," Renee said. She was standing in the doorway, herself wearing one of Karen's long slim wool couture skirts in dark brown. I mean, *moccachino*. "It's a fucking mess."

"You make it sound like it's my fault."

"It is your fault. It's your office."

"Well, I'm sorry that I'm not as pathologically neat and organized as you are."

"You should be."

Renee had been extra sweet to me ever since the denouement with Malcolm. Not that she felt responsible for the breakup, because she didn't. Yes, she was sorry I was sad, but she wasn't sorry the conversation had taken place. In her mind, I was better off knowing where I stood with him. And if that meant I was alone now, then so be it. "At least you're not wasting your time anymore," she'd said. And as usual, she was right. Intellectually, anyway. Loneliness and loss might not have made logical sense, but that didn't make those feelings any less real to me then.

I looked at my watch and then at the pile of proofs I'd just gotten back from the photographer for our fall promotional materials; it was two minutes past eleven, and Karen was waiting for us. "Listen. Let's just get this over with, and then we can talk about—"

"What a slob you are."

"And what an obsessive-compulsive you are."

When we got to Karen's office, she was on the phone. She waved us in, and we sat down in the two guest chairs on the opposite side of her desk.

"Uh-huh. And that was, what, an hour ago? So what's her temperature now?" Karen took a long sip of water from her glass and reached for the small tin of Altoids she kept by the phone. She popped a mint into her mouth but spit it out into the palm of her hand the minute she got her answer. "Around a hundred and three? What do you mean, *around* a hundred and three? Aren't you using the electronic thermometer?"

The expression on Renee's face indicated that the last place on earth she'd want to be was on the other end of that phone line being grilled by Karen as her nanny apparently was. I couldn't have agreed more.

"Listen to me," Karen barked. "The electronic thermometer is *not* too difficult to use. I'm going to hold on while you get it out of the medicine cabinet in Arthur's bathroom, and then I'm going to tell you exactly what to do. I want to know *exactly* what her temperature is." She glanced at us absently, then returned her attention to the nanny—explaining, in great detail, what button to press and what beep to listen for and where to look for the temperature reading. A few seconds passed while the nanny presumably followed the instructions, and then Karen gasped.

"A hundred and *five*? Oh, my God. I'm on my way." She sprang out of her chair, grabbed her coat and bag, and ran out. When she flew by Simon's desk toward the elevator without breaking stride, I regretted all the times I'd been scornful of her as a parent. Certainly Karen was no earth-mother type and never would be, but in her own way she clearly cared about her little girl a great deal. That much anyone could have seen from the look of absolute terror on her face as she raced out the door.

SOMETIME AFTER THREE o'clock that afternoon, Simon appeared in my doorway clutching his heart.

"Did you hear about Marissa?" he asked dramatically.

I put down the plastic sheets of slides I had been looking at. "No. I mean, yes. She had a fever earlier."

Simon pulled a cigarette from the box of Dunhills he kept in his jacket pocket, but his hands were shaking so much as he tried to flick his lighter that he gave up and dropped the unlit cigarette down on my desk. "Marissa had a febrile seizure."

"A what?"

"A febrile seizure. *Febrile:* from the Latin for 'fever.' It's a seizure caused by a fever that spikes too quickly in an infant."

"Oh, my God."

"Poor, poor, *poor* Karen. She just called. She was on the phone with the pediatrician when the child started to, well, *seize.*"

What a terrible word that was.

"Her eyes rolled back in her head, and she began to convulse—her limbs jerking this way and that. Then her breathing became so shallow that Karen actually thought Marissa was dying right there and then! Can you imagine?"

No. I couldn't.

"The doctor called 911, and paramedics arrived on the scene in mere minutes. They got the fever down immediately with cool compresses, and then they took her to the emergency ward for observation. They're home now, thank goodness."

"So how is she?"

"Karen or Marissa?"

"Either. Both."

He reached for his cigarette and lit it, finally. "Marissa is absolutely fine. I called my mother, and she said this sort of thing is quite normal—she was a nurse, you know. And if it's rectified in time, which it was, there are no lasting effects."

"You mean, like—"

"Yes."

Brain damage, neither of us wanted to say.

"And Karen?"

"She's quite shaken," he said, leaning into my desk. "I've never heard her sound so—so frightened. Usually she's, well, you know, impervious to this kind of thing."

"Well, it's not like this kind of thing has ever happened before."

"No, of course not. But she's had me cancel everything for the rest of the week because she wants to be home. Karen has never canceled the rest of any week. Except, of course, when she gave birth." He stubbed his cigarette out. "Which I hope doesn't happen anytime soon. After all, a scare like this can't be good for someone who's seven and a half months pregnant."

I was haunted by the incident for the rest of the day. The mere idea of something happening to my Pickle made my brain shut down from fear. I even called Lynn to reassure myself that everything there was okay.

"How frightening," Lynn said when I told her about Karen's scare. "I don't even want to think about it."

"Me, either."

"But children are incredibly resilient," she said.

"They are?"

"Of course they are. You were."

"When?"

"When your appendix ruptured. You could have died, but you didn't. Remember?"

Of course I remembered. I was four years old; there was a raging blizzard the night my stomach started hurting; and by the time morning came and my parents realized something was really wrong with me, the ambulance had a hard time getting through the storm. But they made it, and I made it, and while Lynn had made me feel better temporarily, I still couldn't help feeling shaken. Life was so fragile, so dangerous, so precarious. Especially a child's life. And it made me wonder if I would be strong enough to handle such a thing were I to have a child of my own—a moment when life and death were all too closely linked.

Later that night as I lay in bed unable to fall asleep, I wondered how Malcolm could have survived losing Benjamin. I had often wondered about that while we were still together—wondered how he had endured the fear all those months and years while his little boy was sick and in and out of the hospital, and then how he'd endured the loss and grief after it was all over—but I'd never actually asked him. The thought of what he had lived through—and what he lived with every day since then—made my eyes fill with tears, and I ached to hear his voice. I realized, suddenly, that I had never told him how sorry I was about Benjamin, and it seemed inconceivable to me that I could have known him as long as I had without ever saying that. I reached across the bed for the phone, but as I held the receiver in my hand, I had no idea of what I would say and where I would start. He and I had not spoken since that terrible night and while I'd had the urge to call him countless times since then, I had always suppressed it. A weepy, wordless, late-night conversation wouldn't change anything, nor would it do either of us any good. So I went to my dresser and got the Big Bird Nicole had given me out of the drawer. And putting it in bed next to me, I finally fell asleep.

I HAD PLANNED on renting a car (I was transporting gifts after all: lingerie for Lynn despite her squawking and an easel and tempera paints for the Pickle) and driving the five hours up to my sister's that Friday afternoon—the day before her birthday—and driving back to the city Monday evening. Despite the residue of the previous day's trauma and the fact that Karen was still out of the office, she and I had spoken several times on the phone, and due to her distraction she had, miraculously, not asked me to change my plans.

Simon, on the other hand, was on the verge of a nervous breakdown. Even though I was only going to be out of the office for a day and a half, to Simon I might as well have been going on a three-month cruise to Alaska.

"I know, I know, I know," I said, swatting him away the day before I left.

"You only have thirty days left to get Karen's gift," he wailed, practically in tears.

"That's four weeks—four and a half weeks. Jesus Christ, they probably built the bomb in less time than that."

He kept his eyes glued to me as if I might fly out the window and vanish without ever getting the present.

"So?"

I stared at him. *"So?"*

"So what are your thoughts? Your ideas? The whole event absolutely *hinges* on the gift, and if there *is* no gift, well, I don't even want to *think* about that scenario right now."

"There'll be a gift, Simon. Don't worry."

He looked at me as if I'd just told him that Santa Claus and the tooth fairy really did exist and that they'd both RSVP'd "yes" to the shower. "There will be? Oh, joy! Do tell me what it is!"

"I haven't decided yet," I said, hoping to intimate that there existed a limited though fabulous selection of items from which I would soon choose.

His excitement grew. "Well, what have you narrowed it down to?"

"A few things," I lied.

Nothing.

Nothing.

Or nothing.

"I'm going to think about it while I'm in Maine, and then I'll make my decision when I get back."

"Then I'll have something to look forward to. I *love* surprises."

LYNN, HOWEVER, HAD never liked surprises—especially surprise birthday parties and especially when she was turning thirty-eight and almost five months pregnant—and so nothing about my impending visit and the celebratory dinner Paul and I had planned for her and Nicole had been kept secret.

The Pickle, she said, when I called her from a rest stop somewhere in Connecticut late Friday afternoon, was beside herself with excitement, even though Lynn wasn't sure whether she understood that it was also her birthday (Lynn's), and not just her own (Nicole's).

"The only thing that matters is that you're coming, and that we're having cake. *Bur-day* cake."

"Don't tell me you're making your own. Bur-day girls aren't supposed to make their own bur-day cakes."

"No no no," she said. "Paul ordered one from Petula's in town. That's your big outing tomorrow afternoon. After you pick up the balloos."

"Ball*oos?*"

"Ball*oons.* Besides a visit from her Auntie LaLa, that's the most exciting part about her turning four."

THE NEXT MORNING I awoke to the sound of heavy breathing in my face. I opened my eyes and saw the Pickle staring at me intently.

"Auntie LaLa," she said.

"Hhhmmm," I said, then closed my eyes.

"Auntie LaLa!"

I opened my eyes again.

"Guess what, Auntie LaLa?"

"What?"

"We're going to have bur-day cake!"

I smiled, still half-asleep. "I know!"

"And you know what else?"

"What?"

"We're going to have balloooooos!"

"I know!"

She put her little hands over my mouth and giggled. "Because you know why?"

"Why?" I tried to say under her fingers.

"Because it's my bur-day."

"Yes, it is!"

"And you know what else?"

"What?"

"It's Mum-Mum's bur-day, too."

"That's right!" See? She did know. "Hey, you know what else?" I asked.

"What?"

I winked at Lynn. "It's my bur-day, too."

"No way!" she said, giggling again.

"Yes way!"

"No way!"

"Yes way!"

Just then Lynn appeared in the doorway, and Nicole ran to her. She picked her daughter up, and Nicole grabbed Lynn's nose with her hand. When she threw her head back, the giggle she let out was so contagious, we all started laughing. "It's not your bur-day, Auntie LaLa, it's Mum-Mum's bur-day and my bur-day!"

"Come on, you two," Lynn said, putting Nicole down and giving her a fake spank on her Pull-Up. "Daddy's waiting to go to the bakery with you to pick up the bur-day cake."

BUR-DAY CAKE AND *balloooos!*

After breakfast the Pickle must have repeated that a thousand times in the few minutes it took Paul to strap her into the car seat of their dark green Jeep Cherokee—let alone when we were actually in the car driving.

First we stopped at the party store to pick up the balloons (pre-balloo-pickup word-repetition count: 312). Then we headed back into town and stopped at the bakery (pre-bur-day-cake-pickup word-repetition count: 688). And once we'd found a parking space and were all unbuckled and unstrapped from our seats, we went inside.

The bakery was warm, and the windows were foggy. I went up to the counter and got in line while Paul and Nicole explored the store. The line was long, and when it failed to move even an inch in five minutes, I found myself getting edgy—me being the tense, uptight, high-strung psycho in from New York for a weekend. Nicole, who was now frantically pointing to gingerbread cookies at the far end of the glass case, didn't seem to be doing too much better mood-wise than I was.

More time passed before I made it up to the front of the line, but when I asked for the cake, I was told they still needed to box it. Annoyed, I stepped out of the line to wait and was soon joined by my niece and her slightly frazzled father.

"Auntie LaLa. I have to pee."

"Really?" I gave a cursory look around the bakery for a rest room sign but didn't see one. "Okay. In just a minute."

"But Auntie LaLa—I have to pee really bad and a lot and a lot."

"I know, honey. Daddy and Auntie LaLa are just going to look at the cake and then we'll find you a bathroom. Okay?"

Before she answered me, the counter girl returned with a pink cardboard box, which she put on the counter and opened for our inspection. Inside was an elaborately frosted sheet cake—pink on white, with the inscription written in the center.

I stared at the cake.

"'Happy Birthday Nicole and Mammo,'" I said, reading the ornate trail of pink calligraphy icing.

Who the hell is *Mammo*?

I turned to Paul, whose head, too, was now inside the box.

"Who's Mammo?" I asked.

"What are you, some kind of ignoramus? You've never heard of Mammo, the Celtic fertility goddess?"

For a split second I believed him. "Really?"

"No." He looked equally confused. "I have no idea."

"What was it supposed to say?"

"Happy Birthday Mum-Mum. You know, what Nicole calls her."

He and I got out from under the top flap of the box and blinked at the girl.

"Do you want us to fix it?" she asked. "It'll be easy to fix—it would just take a few minutes."

Nicole was tugging at my sleeve and then at Paul's, but we'd been too distracted by the frosting fiasco to pay attention. Until we heard the faint sound of trickling water. I finally looked away from the cake and saw Nicole standing between us, whimpering.

"Oh, no!" Her leggings were wet, plus I realized that in our rush to leave this morning, we'd forgotten to put on a Pull-Up. "It's all Auntie LaLa's fault! I forgot you said you had to pee!" I knelt down on the floor and hugged her while Paul grabbed a handful of napkins from the counter and wiped up the floor. Then I stood up and took her little hand in mine.

"Let's go," I said to Paul as he fit the box top into its side panels and put the whole thing under his arm like a small child. "The Pickle needs her Mammo."

· · ·

THAT NIGHT, AFTER Lynn and Paul and I had our grilled
salmon fillets and our rice and our salads, and after Nicole had
had her chicken nuggets, I went into the kitchen and stuck
candles into the cake and carried it back out into the dining
room. Lynn crouched down next to Nicole, and they both
closed their eyes. "Please let me gain only twenty-five pounds
this pregnancy," Lynn said. "Please make my baby-brain go
away and return to normal. Please help me find sweatpants
that make me look thin and that come in black." Then they
blew the candles out. Nicole sang "Hap Bur-day"—her ren-
dition of the old classic—and after we'd explained the typo-
graphical frosting error to Lynn and had a good laugh about
it, I found myself focusing on the cake.

Mammo.

There was something about that word.

I stared at it a bit longer and repeated it to myself a few
more times, hoping I could articulate my sudden fascination
with it:

Mammo.

Mammo.

Mammo.

It looked and sounded vaguely superhero-ish, as if
Mammo could be a comic book character or an animated
Saturday-morning cartoon series or a major motion picture
starring the next Christopher Reeve.

Mammo!

I looked again, and a vision of a semi-flabby woman in a
too-tight blue Lycra body-suit popped into my head.

Then red go-go boots.

Then a flowing cape flapping in the breeze.

Then a big red M on her chest.

Mammo!

Flying from home to preschool to job to supermarket to home again, this wasn't a bird.

Or a plane.

Or Superwoman.

Or Wonder Woman.

This wasn't someone without stretch marks or baby-flab or baby-brain.

This was *Mammo!*

Someone slower than a speeding bullet!

Less powerful than a locomotive!

Unable to leap tall buildings in a single bound!

Someone who knew she couldn't be everywhere and do everything and wear anything other than sweatpants while she was trying and failing!

Someone like Karen who had one kid and one nanny, or someone like Lynn who would have two kids and no nanny—or someone like me who might have one sperm-bank baby and no hud-band or Big Bird. Someone who was strong and proud and fierce and determined and maternalistic and feministic and exhausted and sleep deprived all at once, all the time—someone who hadn't gotten her figure back yet and, quite frankly, didn't care!

Up in the sky, it wasn't a bird! Or a plane!

It was Karen!

It was Lynn!

It was me!

It was Mammo!

I WAS BACK in the office that Tuesday morning, having gotten home late the night before, and though I was exhausted from the drive, I felt as if a huge weight had been lifted off my head.

I had figured out Karen's gift, finally.

Now all I had to do was explain it to Renee and get her to help me with it.

"Oh, my God," she said, straightening up a pile of suit sketches that were on her drawing table. "Simon's going to be so relieved. You should have seen him yesterday—calling Gail and telling on you because you've been so *negligent* in your *duties.*" She headed out of the kitchen toward her office, and I followed. "So what did he think when you told him?"

"Told him? I haven't actually told him. I don't want him to know what it is yet."

"Why not?"

"It's not exactly something that's store-bought. It's a little conceptual, so it's kind of hard to describe."

She smacked a new pack of Marlboros against the palm of her hand, then tore off the plastic. "What is it?"

"Well, it *isn't* yet. It's, you know, it has to be made."

"*Custom* made?"

"Yeah. Sort of."

She was rapidly losing patience with my evasiveness. "What the fuck is it already? I don't have all day."

"Okay."

I planted both feet on the floor and made my hands into a frame as if I were one of those cheesy Hollywood producers about to pitch a one-word concept movie:

"*Mammo!*"

"Excuse me?" she said.

I got into position and repeated my karate-chop stance.

"*Mammo!*" I said again.

Renee looked at me as if I were a madwoman.

"I have no idea what you're talking about."

I could see I was going to have to start from scratch.

"You know how all these women who become mothers

are always conflicted and tormented about everything? They love being mothers, and they love being home with their kids, cooking and baking and playing with Play-Doh and watching *Barney* with them, but they also feel kind of guilty about liking it? As if they shouldn't be such losers and should be back at work and back in shape like they were before they had their babies?"

"Yeah? So?"

"And the ones who do go back to work feel guilty about that, too, because they think they should be home with their kids, cooking and baking and playing with Play-Doh and watching *Barney* with them, instead of sitting at their desks till seven o'clock at night working like maniacs and afraid they're going to get fired?"

"Like I said the first time: Yeah? So?"

"Ergo *Mammo!*"

Silence.

"Where'd you come up with this brainstorm?"

"In Maine."

"In Maine, huh? What's the official state bird up there, the white-tailed asswipe?"

"Is it that bad?" I asked, not really wanting to hear her answer.

"I don't know yet. Keep talking."

"Mammo is pride. Conviction. Strength. Self-assurance. Whether you're married with children, or unmarried with children."

She crossed her arms and shifted her weight onto her other leg. She was intrigued, even though I could tell she was pretending not to be.

"Mammo isn't just a mom, she's"—I lifted my shoulders and stuck my arms out in frustration over being so inarticulate—"she's—*Mammo!*"

Renee nodded, finally.

"Okay. That's kind of interesting. Now what does it have to do with Karen's gift?"

"It *is* the gift. Mammo on a necklace—in silver letters—on a thin cord—like a choker." I pointed to the bone at the base of my neck, where I envisioned it would rest. "*Mammo* the word, the necklace, the idea—is Mother Power. Ipso facto."

I paused again for dramatic effect.

"See? Mammo—Mother Power—for Karen. For a woman who, despite herself, embodies that."

She lit a cigarette and thought about it for a second or two.

"It's a little high-concept," she finally said.

"Do you think she'll get it?"

Renee raised an eyebrow. "She invented high-concept."

"But what do you think?" I demanded.

"What do *I* think? I think you're weird."

She sounded like my mother. "I know you think I'm weird, but what do you think about the idea? About the necklace?"

"I think you want the necklace for yourself because *you* want to be a Mammo."

I laughed.

"Am I wrong?" she said.

I laughed again. "No. You're not wrong. You're never wrong, Renee."

"Of course I'm not." She threw her arm over my shoulders and walked me to the door. "Now get away from me so I can start thinking about your stupid necklace, so you can walk around wearing it and pretending you have a kid."

RENEE AGREED TO design a prototype of the necklace—a rough sketch and specs on material and font style and size and cord length— so we could take it to a jewelry designer to have it made. Every time she saw me for the rest of the day, she complained about how busy she was and how much more work she had to do than I did, which wasn't even true. But the next morning she walked by my office with her big black leather portfolio and indicated that I should follow her to her office.

"Hey, Mammo," she said with her sunglasses still on and barely slowing down as she passed my door, "get in here."

I jumped up from my desk and ran into her office with my coffee and shut the door.

"It's very rough," she said, hovering over me as I looked at the sketch on her desk. For all her bluff and bluster, she was a completely insecure perfectionist who wanted everything she designed to be brilliant on the first try. Which it usually was.

I stepped back from her desk.

"Could you move your hair? I can barely see," I said, then moved back to take in the drawing she'd laid out on the table. Seeing the word *Mammo* displayed for the first time since the accidental birthday cake inscription gave me a thrill.

Renee lit a cigarette and began to pace around her office, waiting for me to make my pronouncement.

"It's great!" I said. "It's amazing! It's exactly what I'd imagined!"

"Only better." She was smiling now, and relieved. She walked back to her drawing table and adjusted the lamp above it. "I really like this font," she said. "It's a clean, basic, no-nonsense type. Like the word and the person it describes."

"Good," I said.

"I used all lowercase letters, like typewriter-type, because I think that also serves to get the point across. It reinforces the idea of Mammo as a professional woman, yet it's understated."

"Good," I said again, staring at how the word looked in its new typeface:

mammo.

I liked it.

"Now for materials." She looked at me and squinted at the line of smoke that had just gone straight into her eye. "Since this is for Karen—the woman who has everything and hates everything unless she's designed it—the materials have to be the best."

"So not sterling silver."

She shook her head.

"What about eighteen-karat gold?"

"Her upper lip curled. "I don't think so."

"Twenty-four-karat gold?"

Nope.

"White gold?"

Nope.

"What's left?"

"Platinum."

"Platinum? Jesus. How much will that cost?"

"A fortune." She closed her pad and stubbed her cigarette out. "Don't worry yet. I've got a friend who's a jewelry designer in SoHo, and she has a friend in the jewelry district—and they both love Karen's clothes. Let's see if they'd do a trade."

"Yeah, right. One piece of platinum for five suits."

"For five hundred suits."

THE FOLLOWING AFTERNOON Renee told me that she'd faxed the mammo sketches to her friend downtown, who was going to get started on designing the necklace right away. Both she and her platinum-pimping associate, she said, would work with us on a trade: service and materials for clothes.

Renee had worked out a rough barter with Annette for Karen Lipps Green Label sample suits and a range of other KLNY merchandise—shoes and sweaters and sunglasses and outerwear, and the rest, she said, I'd have to figure out.

"Chisel open that discretionary promotional budget of yours," she said. "Or get Simon to chisel open his petty cash budget—Karen makes him spend about twenty-five thousand dollars a day on bottled water, so she'd probably never even miss it anyway."

She told me we'd see the necklace in about two weeks, have a few days to make changes, and then the designer would need another week to finalize it.

"So unless she dies or something horrible happens to her between now and then, you'll have your stupid necklace by April twenty-fifth."

Which would, according to Simon's hyperprecise calculations, leave only five days to wrap it.

15

. . .

AN AERIAL VIEW of the elaborate automative choreography necessary to transport two hundred Very Important Women out of New York City to the south fork of Long Island on a Sunday morning in May would make Operation Desert Storm look like a walk in the park.

On the day of Karen's shower, black hired sedans, limousines, and chauffeured cars with tinted windows would begin making their scheduled pickups at ten A.M. at various exclusive and often highly guarded addresses around town— mostly on Fifth Avenue, Madison Avenue, Park Avenue, Central Park West, and Central Park South; a few in SoHo and one or two in TriBeCa—their minibars and backseats stocked with the prerequested necessities of bottled water, diet soda, fruit, and newspapers and magazines, not to mention special lower-lumbar back pillows and the occasional blanket. Fanning out in formation around the city toward the Triborough Bridge and beyond, their cranky and demanding celebrity cargo would be complaining constantly in the backseats about the lack of air or too much of it, since any true New Yorker is loath ever to leave the city, unless it's to go to the Hamptons, and then, well, they still hate to make the trip.

Even Karen, the guest of honor, who by now was eight and a half months pregnant and uncomfortably big, was dreading it. Not only could she have used that Sunday afternoon in the office (she was still making up for the days she'd taken off following Marissa's illness), but she also hated surprises. She knew that there was a gift coming to her from the staff, but she still didn't know what it was—and that was driving her crazy.

"Hi. It's me. Did I wake you?"

Karen.

I looked at the clock: *seven-thirty.*

I'd actually been up since five-thirty, trying to figure out how to tie the Lipps-red organza ribbon around the mammo necklace box the way professional gift wrappers did, until I gave up and called Simon at six. He'd walked me through the cutting and threading and tying over the phone like an emergency quadruple bypass.

"Listen," said Karen, without the pretense of waiting for my reply or apologizing for calling so early. She and I had known each other long enough to be beyond such formalities. "What's the gift you're all giving me? I know you're in charge of it."

"It's a surprise."

"I hate surprises, you know that. I tried to get it out of Simon all week, but I couldn't crack him."

An image of Simon held captive by Karen in one of her white upholstered office chairs for hours and hours and refusing to talk flashed into my mind.

"Well, you know how good he is at keeping secrets." Especially when he doesn't even know the secret.

"Bullshit. He's the biggest gossip in the business. How do

you think the columns know where I'm eating and what I'm eating every minute of every day?"

So Simon was the leak!

"Anyway, what is it?" I could hear the impatience growing in her voice. "Ellen, listen. I just want to know what the gift is before I open it. You may not know this about me, but sometimes I have trouble hiding my feelings if I don't like something."

"I understand. Really, I do. But I just don't feel right about telling. I mean, I haven't told anyone—including Simon—what it is." Only Renee had seen it, late on Friday afternoon when the finished necklace came back finally from the designer. "It would ruin everything for Simon—not to mention the rest of the staff—if I were to spoil the surprise."

"But why is it such a secret?"

"I can't tell you that."

"Then give me a hint. Was Arthur in on it?"

"No."

"Gail?"

"No."

"Is it something for the nursery? Furniture or bedding or another one of those goddamned black-and-white visually contrasting mobiles to hang over the crib? Or is it something to wear?"

"Kind of."

"Ellen, please." She was getting exasperated, and I knew I didn't have much room left to play around with. "What do you mean, 'kind of'?"

"Okay. It's something to wear."

"Clothes?"

I stopped myself from saying *kind of* again and responded with a definitive lie:

"Yes. It's clothes. Baby clothes."

"Finally. Now listen, when are you leaving for the country?"

The country. Only in Manhattan were the Hamptons considered the country.

"Around nine. I'm picking Renee up first. We're going out there early to help with whatever last-minute things need to be done."

"Gail doesn't need any help. She's had most of Martha's people up there since yesterday. I'll call her and tell her you're not coming early and that we'll be there at noon. My car is coming to get me at nine-thirty. Tell Renee to be at your building at nine-forty-five, and I'll pick the two of you up so we can all go together."

I WAS STILL running around my apartment like a maniac when the doorman called to tell me that Renee had arrived. I went downstairs to the lobby, only to turn around once I'd gotten there when I realized I'd forgotten the gift.

Clearly annoyed that she had to be doing anything on a Sunday that involved work and annoyed that we were dressed almost identically in our spring-weight black KLNY capri pants and cardigan twin sets, Renee told me I should go up and change.

"I'm not changing," I said.

"Why not? We look like we both work at Bendel's." Her voice was heavy with disdain. Renee hated Bendel's because she thought their stores and their merchandise were too aggressively cute and because they didn't sell men's clothes. The fact that Karen had once designed for them had always been a sore spot for her.

"Because there's no time. And besides, what would I change into? Everything I own is a variation of this." I grabbed at my sweater and pulled on it with frustration. "It's not like I'm going to go up there, and something pink or green is suddenly going to materialize. The best I'll do is find something that's a different shade of black."

She rummaged through her bag for a cigarette, then swore under her breath when she realized she was out. "Fine. We look like asswipes. I'm going over to the newsstand to get a pack of cigarettes." She walked off in a huff and returned two minutes later in mid-smoke. When Karen's driver pulled up in front of my building, Renee put her sunglasses on and pushed me away from the door to the front seat.

"You're sitting in back with her," she ordered.

TWO AND A half hours and about a thousand dollars' worth of cell phone calls each later, we reached our destination—East Hampton—and Gail's expansive white Victorian house, which looked as if it had been transformed over the last twenty-four hours into something out of, well, out of a Martha Stewart book.

We pulled into the long gravel driveway, and as the tires crunched along slowly, the three of us sat in silence behind our tinted windows and our sunglasses and took in the scene. Industry people we knew from other design houses and from magazines and retailers were there, as were celebrities and their car-and-driver-entourages. Waiters were already trickling out of the house and onto the lawn with small round trays of sweating champagne flutes.

"I have *got* to pee," Karen said, squirming beside me. But she kept her eyes on the Who's Who of Women milling around on the lawn, as did I: Barbara Walters, Nora Ephron, Lynda Obst, Cindy Crawford, Carly Simon, Katie Couric, Anna Wintour, Donna Karan, Vera Wang, Esther Dyson, Tina Brown, Kim Basinger, Winona Ryder, Gwyneth Paltrow, Liz

Smith, Brooke Astor, Jane Pauley, Anna Deavere Smith, Maria Shriver, Binky Urban, Esther Newburg, Kathy Robbins, Lynn Nesbit, Helen Gurley Brown, Gail Sheehy, Katharine Graham, Joni Evans, Erica Jong, Donna Shalala, Rosie O'Donnell, and Susan Sarandon—to name only thirty-one.

And the car hadn't even come to a complete stop yet.

And I wasn't even counting Arlene Schiffler.

Karen's driver pulled around the semicircular driveway in front of the house and stopped just short of the stone steps that led up to the wraparound porch. The three of us stepped out into the bright sunshine, and as Karen took the lead, Renee and I flanked her on either side, the way Secret Service agents flank the President in the protective V formation. A look of gratitude appeared in Karen's eyes the instant before she turned and headed into the eye of the storm.

In less time than it takes for atoms to collide and release their energy, an epic and gruesome display of air-kissing and ass-kissing erupted as Karen made her way to the house. Even after almost eight years in the business, I still hadn't gotten used to such blatant hypocrisy: everybody there hated at least one other person there (if not ten other people). More than a few of Karen's enemies had even been invited, and not only had they shown up, but they'd come bearing hugs and kisses and extravagantly wrapped gifts.

Renee and I immediately extricated ourselves from the crush of bodies and flesh and clashing fragrances and headed up to the porch as quickly as we could, Renee in search of the stiffest drink she could find ("Champagne? *Please.* I need a vodka"), and me, of course, in search of Simon.

There were flowers everywhere, lining the path to the house, dripping down over the doors in garlands and exploding out of window boxes. The front door was open, and through it I could see more flowers—a big huge arrangement in the center of the foyer, for starters. Gail was in the doorway, a one-woman receiving line, busily greeting guests—or actually, introducing herself to guests, since she didn't know most of them. When I kissed her hello, she somehow had the presence of mind, despite the chaos and excitement going on around her, to point to Karen's ass and then whisper in my ear that it was, of course, hidden up against one of the pillars on the veranda.

"Why should today be any different from every other day?" she said, before introducing herself to Cindy Adams.

When I finally found Simon, he was sitting on the stuffed arm of a thickly padded club chair in the living room and chatting away with Arlene Schiffler. Most of the guests were still out on the lawn, and a few suburban friends of Gail's, who clearly looked as if they felt out of place, made quiet small talk along the edges of the room. As I approached, he smiled beatifically.

"Here she is," he announced as he stood and bowed. "The gift goddess." He took my hand and brought it to his mouth, but I retracted it quickly. "The gift she's selected is apparently *so* fabulous, she wouldn't even tell *me* what it is—even though everybody *knows* I guard the Queen's secrets as if they were my own."

I smiled to myself when I saw Simon's eyes zeroing in on Karen like a heat-seeking missile. I followed his line of vision to find her standing by the staircase, waving away a tray of hors d'oeuvres being passed in front of her. Instinctively, his hand moved to caress the faint outline of a cell phone tucked away in his breast pocket, only a speed-dial away from calling in his observations to whichever columnist he'd predetermined would be waiting on the other end.

"I feel as if this shower were somehow meant for me, too," Arlene said, "as I'm due in twelve weeks." I hadn't seen her in the flesh for at least two years—and certainly not

since her column began—something I was grateful for—
and I tried to hide my displeasure at having to see her at all.
Even six months pregnant she looked stunning—tall, fit,
implausibly unbloated, not a butterscotch-colored hair out
of place. I wanted to hit her. But instead I pointed at her
protruding stomach beneath her blazer and decided to torture her.

"God, you're *huge!*"

"No, I'm not!"

"Yes! You are!" I turned to Simon, who was still focused
on Karen. "Isn't she just *huge?*"

"I'll say," he said.

"I've only gained seventeen pounds."

"Seventeen pounds! Wow! Isn't it weird how you can gain
so much weight when the fetus is still only, like, two
pounds?"

"My doctor says seventeen pounds is unbelievably low."

"Well, of course he'd say that. He's not the one carrying
them around. Besides, he probably didn't want you to
worry."

"Worry about what?"

"About never taking the weight off."

"I'm not worried," she said.

Liar.

"Good."

"I mean, I know this sounds incredibly narcissistic, but the
minute I deliver, I'm going off to a spa. I think it's crucial for
women to reclaim their bodies as quickly after giving birth
as possible."

I nodded, having read all about it in her column, "Month
Four."

"Unlike Karen." She craned her neck to look past Simon.
"I mean, look what the whale dragged in."

Maybe it was because I disliked Arlene so much, or maybe

it was because of Karen's recent scare with Marissa, but I suddenly felt protective of my impossible boss.

"Expectant mammos are supposed to be big. You know, because they're eating for two. Because they're eating to give life to someone else. That's what being pregnant means."

Before I realized the slip I'd made, Arlene choked on an ice cube and started coughing so hard, I thought she might risk undoing her *cerclage* ("Month Five"). But after Simon patted her on the back until she'd recovered, she flipped open her steno pad and started scribbling.

"I keep forgetting," she said, looking around the room for "material" to jot down. "I'm a journalist *and* a mother-to-be."

And an asswipe, I wanted to say before excusing myself to look for Renee.

When I finally found her in the back of the living room, she was flirting with a bartender, who apparently was gay, since she mouthed the word "fag" at me as I approached. She pulled me to her by the elbow so she could whisper as loudly as she could into my hair.

"Can we leave yet? I hate baby showers."

"I know you do."

"But let me clarify that statement: I don't hate babies."

"I know you don't."

"How do you know that?"

"Because I know that underneath it all, you're a big softie." And she was. Especially when she was drunk.

"Don't get carried away. I'm not that nice."

"Yes, you are. In spite of yourself."

"I just never wanted them—kids. Maybe I would have if one of my relationships had ever worked out. But none of my relationships ever worked out."

"You'll have a relationship that'll work out," I said.

"No, I won't. It's too late. And I'm too old."

"It is not, and you are not."

She threw her arm around me, and it landed on my shoulders with a heavy thud. "You think?"

"I know."

"Maybe you'll get back together with that impoholic of yours and have a kid, or maybe you'll find someone better to have a kid with."

A month had passed, and Malcolm and I hadn't even spoken on the phone, so it seemed highly unlikely that a reunion was imminent, or possible. I'd even forced myself to disconnect the Caller ID box to train myself to stop thinking that he might call. And as far as my finding someone better—well, that looked equally unlikely, since I worked in a female- and gay-male-dominated industry. Not to mention that this was a party for mostly women.

"Maybe."

"We've had our heart-to-heart, so *now* can we go?"

"Of course we can't," I said, and being two very visible members of Karen's staff, we tacitly resigned ourselves to staying and suffering.

The first interminable hour was mercifully coming to a close, which was a relief since now there was the complete distraction of food instead of only the partial distraction of hors d'oeuvres. Gail's huge dining room had been transformed into one big food station, with silver platters of hams and roasted turkeys and whole poached salmons; stone bowls filled with salads and side dishes; and wicker baskets stuffed with breads and muffins and every other kind of baked good imaginable. The sound of china and silverware clanging and people oohing and aahing over the buffet— even though most of these women never ate anything anyway—filled the air, until the decibel level was such that ten jets could have taken off and landed in the living room and no one would have noticed.

Once the food had been picked at, and the dishes were cleared, and coffee and finger pastries had been laid out and ignored, the moment Simon had been waiting for since January was close at hand. I could see Karen a few feet away, sitting in a huge stuffed armchair—like a Buddha—and then I saw Gail make her way through the crowd to Karen and whisper something in her ear—presumably that the gift-giving ceremony would soon begin. Gail then began to spread the word to those standing closest to her, and within minutes a space was cleared in a semicircle around Karen, and the wait staff began carrying in the gifts and laying them in a huge pile at her feet.

Which meant it was time to find Simon.

I FOUND HIM in the kitchen, standing in the pantry flapping his arms like a chicken and flipping his hair out of his face so emphatically, he was practically hitting himself. I didn't know exactly what the problem was, but I certainly knew we had one.

"I've just been informed that Celine's not coming, so there's no one to sing, and," he said, as if the worst were yet to come, "we've forgotten something. Something incredibly fundamentally relevant to this day."

I pointed to my KLNY microfiber tote bag attached to my shoulder like a third arm.

"What are you panicking for? I've got it."

"You *do*? You've got a *card*???"

"What card? I'm talking about the gift. The gift you've been torturing me about the past five months."

He put his fingers to his temples and pressed in for a second or two before speaking. "Ellen, we don't have a card."

"Hey. Chicken Little. Who cares about a card when we

have *this!*" I pulled the beribboned little box out of my bag and shoved it in his face.

His eyes lit up. "You're right. The gift *is* the most important thing." His fingers reached out like octopus tentacles, but I pulled back just in time to avoid them, clutching the box protectively to my chest. And before I could continue torturing him, we heard the unmistakable tinkling of crystal stemware and the final announcement coming from the living room:

"Gift time!"

BY THE FIFTIETH gift, even Karen was having a hard time feigning excitement.

Beautifully wrapped box after beautifully wrapped box was passed from Gail to Simon to Karen to be opened—each precious pearl contained within to be held up and beheld—and every time it was, a Greek chorus of oohs and aahs would rise up from the rapt crowd.

Ooooh!

Oshkosh B'Gosh unisex denim overalls and little white turtleneck!

Ahhhh!

A handmade alphabet quilt from Barney's!

Ooooh!

Another handmade alphabet quilt from Barney's!

Ahhhh!

More fabulous miniature silly ridiculously overpriced things from Petit Bateau and Bulgari and Kiehl's and Tiffany!

When all the boxes were finally opened, I saw Simon signal me and Renee and Annette, whom I hadn't seen all morning, and the rest of our office staff: It was time for us to gather around Karen and finally bestow upon our boss our own perfectly wrapped box, too, and to wait and watch breathlessly as she opened it up and said . . .

Nothing.

Absolutely nothing.

She made a face.

She moved her lips in an attempt to pronounce the word but gave up almost instantly.

"It's a *necklace!*" she said, looking out into the sea of familiar staff faces for help while she forced herself to keep smiling. "A *necklace* with a *word* hanging off of it!"

A hushed wave of ooohs and ahhhs undulated through the crowd.

A necklace!

With a word hanging off of it!

I felt sick to my stomach. What could I possibly have been thinking to risk such complete and utter public humiliation by giving Karen such a ridiculous gift?

Simon glared at me and elbowed me to say something. I stood there for a second or two trying to gather my thoughts and hoping to get some silent sign of moral support from Renee, but for once, she was speechless.

Then I looked at Karen. One hand was outstretched with the necklace still dangling from it, while the other hand rested on her stomach protectively. She seemed, for a moment, to have forgotten where she was—forgotten her friends and clients and staff and sister, forgotten the effort to be courteous in the wake of our indecipherable gift. And I suddenly realized that you could never know what was in someone else's heart or mind, no matter how smart you thought you were. Sitting there, smiling even, she looked surprisingly at peace, and buoyed by her quiet contentment, I reached down and plucked the necklace out of Karen's hand and held it up so everyone could see it.

"The necklace says . . . mammo!" I proclaimed dramatically.

Nobody moved.

Or spoke.

Now the *entire* room was silent.

I felt myself starting to sweat and panic, and I realized that I had better do my combination karate-chop stance and Mother Power explanation as quickly as possible and get the hell out of there.

Which I did. And when I was finished, I handed the necklace back to Karen and started to turn away. But before I could, she grabbed my hand. I looked at her nervously and was shocked to see a grin forming on her face.

"That's the most *fantastic* word I've ever heard," Karen pronounced.

I stopped dead in my tracks and stared at her in shock. "You like it?"

"Like it? I *love* it."

I could hear Simon and Renee both breathe sighs of relief, but before we all finished patting each other on the back for a disaster averted, the crowd around us started to part, and a woman appeared, like Moses, in its midst.

Demi Moore.

She came up next to Karen and touched the mammo as it dangled from her fingers, staring at it with the kind of reverence and awe celebrities usually reserve only for staring at themselves.

"What's it made of?" she asked.

Karen nudged me to answer.

"Platinum," I said nervously. I'd never seen Demi Moore—the *Vanity Fair*–anointed Mother of All Mothers—up close before, and I had to say, she was the most beautiful woman I had ever seen.

"And the cord?"

"A special twisted silk thread." I tried desperately to remember what Renee had told me when I hadn't been listening. "It's made in Peru."

"I have to have one."

Karen elbowed me again.

"Okay," I said, completely detached from reality.

"Where did you get it?"

"Well, I . . . it's—I kind of had it made."

"So it's yours."

I nodded.

"So if I asked you, you could have one made for me, too."

I nodded again.

"Do you have a card?"

I reached into my bag and handed her one.

"My assistant will be in touch." She bent down and gave Karen a kiss on the cheek, and then she turned around and walked back into the crowd.

In seconds the women standing around Demi Moore had formed a support group—all of them excitedly talking over each other about their children and stretch marks and weight gain and sex after vaginal deliveries and Mother Power and the need for maternalistic feministic conviction and pride and . . .

mammo mammo mammo

Seconds later the crowd parted again, when Renee wheeled a matching silver-frosted mammo cake toward Karen. But as Karen huffed and puffed trying to extricate herself from the armchair, then finally stood up, those of us close to her heard a strange gushing sound.

And then a high-pitched screech:

"My water just broke!"

The room erupted in cheers and spontaneous applause. Gail ran to her side and helped her through the crowd and toward the bathroom, and Simon, who had been perched on the edge of her chair, suddenly looked green, then white, then completely translucent, until I thought he might collapse in a heap on the floor.

Being a fainter myself, I rushed over to him. And as I did, I noticed Arlene Schiffler, who had been scribbling furiously all afternoon stealing other people's comments and quotes, holding up a hand-held tape recorder into the air to capture the tail end of the mammo comet and sporadically bringing it up to her mouth and talking into it, *reporting everything that happened as it happened!*

Simon stared glassily at me and then at the floor, and then he turned green and white and translucent again.

"Wait until the columns hear about this," he whispered in complete and utter repulsion, pointing at the puddle of amniotic fluid seeping slowly into the antique carpet. "It most certainly will not be *a good thing.*"

16

. . .

KAREN GAVE BIRTH later that evening—at exactly 6:57
P.M.—to an eleven-pound eight-ounce baby boy. Gail had
called an ambulance shortly after Karen's water broke, and
they'd both headed into Manhattan to Mt. Sinai Hospital
where Karen's ob/gyn was waiting. Gail said she would call
Arthur from her cell phone and asked me to stay behind
and deal with the mass exodus of the guests and caterers.
Simon and Annette and Renee stayed behind, too, and
between the four of us, we thanked and said good-bye to
the final hangers-on; oversaw the kitchen staff, who packed
up the leftover food, which was to be donated, as per
Karen's instructions, to two homeless shelters on the Island;
organized the presents, which were still strewn all over the
living-room floor; and made a list of gifts and gift-givers,
so that Simon could get started on the thank-you notes the
next morning.

It was after five by the time we were finished. We called
two cars to take us back to the city—one for Annette, who
wanted to go straight home to Queens, and one for the

three of us to go to the hospital. When Renee and Simon and I arrived at the maternity ward just after eight o'clock, Gail told us the good news: It had been a quick and easy birth (vaginal); mother and newborn were resting comfortably; proud father and little big sister were having a snack in the cafeteria.

I got the phone network in motion—calling a few friends of Gail's and Annette at home and asking them to start making calls, too—and jotted down a few notes for the press release our public relations firm would write and start faxing out early the next morning: the exact time of birth and weight of baby, and the correct spelling of new baby's full name: Eli Daniel Klein.

Sometime after nine, Gail came out again to tell us apologetically that Karen and the baby were too exhausted for visitors. "It's been a long day," she said, and while Renee and I understood and were even relieved—it had been a long day for us, too—Simon's face dropped.

"But—but I simply must see the baby," he said, desperate, I knew, for a few details to feed his waiting columnists.

"Tomorrow," Gail said. "The baby isn't going anywhere."

"Yes, but you see, tomorrow's too late."

"Not for *The New York Observer,*" I said, taking him by the elbow and leading him toward the elevator. "They put the paper to bed on Tuesday."

"NO WONDER SHE was so huge. She didn't have a C-section, did she?" Amy said, her eyes bugging out of her head when I told her about Karen's baby. She and I had had a long-standing dinner date for the Monday night after the shower, and though we hadn't seen that much of each other during my month of racing to the gift finish line, we'd spoken on the phone regularly through it all. By the time we sat down at our favorite booth at L'Acajou, she was dying for the Marv Albert mammo blow-by-blow.

"No. Can you imagine?"

"No. And I don't want to try."

So I told her all about the necklace instead—prebestowal, bestowal, and postbestowal. But when I told her about Karen's surprisingly good reaction and Demi Moore's wanting to order one for herself, she immediately switched into her legal mode.

"You don't want anyone competing with mammo," she said sternly.

"Yeah, like who? The people who invented mammograms?"

"I'm serious. If you protect the word, no one else can use it. Obviously copyright or trademark infringement is not my specialty, but there's someone at my firm who you should talk to."

"Well, maybe, but I really don't think it's going to be an issue."

"Don't be so sure. With Demi Moore running around wearing it, you might very well have a situation on your hands, and if so, it's better to be safe than sorry. Especially if you want to start up a little side business making mammo jewelry in your spare time."

"What spare time?"

DEMI MOORE'S ASSISTANT did call me a few days after Karen's shower to place her boss's order, and she told me, confidentially of course, that Demi was considering doing another naked *Vanity Fair* cover. "Demi thinks wearing only the mammo necklace would be fantastic," she said, in that breathy reverential ironyless way twelve-year-old assistants to famous people do. "She's been looking for a way to promote her being a mother instead of just being pregnant ever since she and Bruce, you know, split up."

Demi wanted one necklace for herself, in platinum natu-rally, with a diamond in the *o* of mammo, and four others for close friends who apparently were "in desperate need of moral support in order to transform themselves from mom-mies into mammos."

But when her assistant asked me how much they'd cost and did I want to take a credit card number now, over the phone, I panicked, told her I'd call back, and ran into Renee's office.

"What am I supposed to do with this order for a gazillion dollars' worth of platinum and diamond necklaces?" I said, still gripping the little scrap of paper I'd written all the informa-tion down on—my pathetic excuse for an order form.

Renee, who'd been holding for someone on the phone when I walked in, hung up immediately.

"How many did she order?"

"Five," I said, then told her the specifics.

Her eyes widened. "The first thing we're going to do is call the designer who made Karen's necklace and tell her to get started on five more. Of course, this time we'll have to pay for them—you know, with *money.*"

"Speaking of money," I interrupted, "how much do we charge for them? A thousand each? Two thousand each?"

She looked at me as if I were an imbecile.

"The *cord* practically cost that much."

"So what then?"

She thought a minute. "I'll call around, but I'm thinking somewhere in the vicinity of fifteen."

"Fifteen *thousand*? For all five, you mean." I started to do a little quick division—*fifteen into five, I mean, five into fifteen was . . . ?*—but before I could finish calculating, she was on me again.

"Fifteen thousand *each*," she said. "Or $12,500 each and $15,000 for the one with the diamond. We'll have to see."

"Are you kidding me?"

"If you charge less, they won't want it."

I knew that.

"You're going to clean up on these, believe me."

And so would she, since she'd helped me design it in the first place.

A FEW DAYS later the necklace was mentioned in *WWD*. It was in an item about Karen's shower and the star-studded guest list of invitees and the shock of her water breaking and the birth of Eli Daniel a few hours later. Then it reported Demi Moore's enthusiastic response to the necklace and the concept behind it, and then the feminista feeding frenzy that ensued.

A week or so later, another mention appeared in *W.*

And then one in *The Intelligencer.*

And on "Page Six."

And in Liz Smith's column.

And in Cindy Adams's column.

And as the mentions in the trades and in the columns came in, so did more orders.

Once or twice a day, Jennifer would buzz to tell me another famous person was on the line calling about mammo—someone who had either been at the shower or who hadn't been at the shower but had heard about it from someone who had been. Or maybe they'd read about it in some newspaper or magazine. One by one the calls came, with women ordering two, sometimes three necklaces at a time for themselves or for their sisters or for their mothers or for their best friends. After a few weeks of running to Renee with my little slips of paper, I was afraid we might have to replace the path of carpeting that ran between our two offices.

Then one morning two weeks later, Jennifer buzzed me with another necklace-related call.

"It's Jay Tipparini III, from Tiffany's?"

"I don't know any Jay Tipparini. Do you?"

"No, but he said it's in reference to mammo?"

I speed-swiveled over to my desk phone and picked up.

"Jay Tipparini III, vice president of marketing and development, Tiffany & Company," he said, as if he were reading his entire business card into the phone.

"Ellen Franck, director of marketing, Karen Lipps New York," I said, idiotically, doing the same.

"Am I correct in assuming that I am speaking to the creator of mammo?" he said.

"Yes."

Me and some anonymous, dyslexic birthday-cake-icer in Maine.

"We'd like to discuss with you some ideas we've had in relation to your aforementioned mammo. At your convenience, of course."

"Right now is a good time."

"Yes, fine." He cleared his throat. "Tiffany & Company has been most impressed by what it has read in the trade publications and columns of late. And we understand that there has been a groundswell of enthusiasm building from Demi Moore's initial order to you for several necklaces— and that quite a few other well-known women have placed orders with you for necklaces as well. As there is talk of Ms. Moore's doing another *Vanity Fair* cover wearing this necklace—and *only* this necklace," he continued, "we are, well, we believe she may inspire other women to follow her lead in this mammo trend as well."

"Really?!" I said, though I was surprised that Tiffany would be aware of—let alone interested in—trendiness.

"Yes, well, we are fully aware of the fact that we, too, along with the rest of the retail world, are in a new millennium, and as we are not able to change that fact, we are looking to become—how shall I say?—more contemporary. To appeal to a younger jewelry-wearing clientele. And so, to that end, we would like to talk with you about an arrangement of sorts."

I blinked. "What kind of arrangement?"

"Well, it's best we save the particulars for a lengthier conversation at our offices, but until then"—he paused before continuing—"we would like to explore the possibility of an exclusive arrangement with Tiffany & Company, through which a complete line of your mammo pieces would be produced and sold. Much in the same way that the lines designed by Paloma Picasso and Elsa Peretti are produced by and sold exclusively through Tiffany."

"Uh-huh, uh-huh," I said, as if I could actually see him paving the way to my financial future. For a second or two between sentences, I suddenly realized what a deal like this could mean:

I could really afford to have a baby.

I could quit my job for a while to raise it.

I felt my stomach drop with excitement and panic, then forced myself to return my full attention to the generous little man inside the phone.

"Perhaps it would be easiest if I put something together in writing—a proposal of sorts," he said.

"Yes. That would be helpful."

"Shall I send it to you directly or to your lawyers?"

"To . . . my lawyer," I said, thinking how funny it sounded. "Amy Jacobs."

. . .

THE FIRST THING I did after my close encounter of the Tiffany's kind was tell Renee, of course.

Then I called Lynn.

And my parents.

And finally I called Amy.

"Remember what you said about protecting mammo in case I wanted to start a little side business?" I then told her about the unbelievable conversation I'd just had with Jay Tipparini.

She and I got together the next day in her office during lunch to go over some research that she and an associate had started to put together—the most important piece of it being that a preliminary title and name search for the word mammo had turned up nothing. This, apparently, in the copyright and intellectual property business, was fabulous news, since it meant that we were free to register mammo as a trademarked product name. Amy told me she'd complete the paperwork in the next few days so we could move on to the next stage of things.

In the meantime the proposal arrived from Tiffany, and when it did, an associate of Amy's, Ward Coakley, went through it. The following week the three of us met in Jay Tipparini's imperial climate-controlled conference chamber high above Fifth Avenue. Introductions were made, seats were taken, proposal papers were passed, and cool water was poured into crystal glasses. Incomprehensible legalese ensued. Which Amy tried to explain to me over drinks immediately afterward across the street at the Oak Room in the Plaza, once we'd parted company with Ward.

I would retain the rights for the mammo word and the design, she told me, and Tiffany would produce the jewelry

and sell it. Their initial proposal would be to make the signature mammo necklace available in several sizes and materials:
sterling silver; eighteen- and twenty-two-karat gold; white
gold; as well as the original platinum. Gemstones such as dia-
monds, rubies, sapphires, and emeralds would be made available upon request. In addition, the mammo series would be
expanded to include a matching ring, a matching bracelet,
matching earrings—studs, most probably—and matching
pen—fountain, roller ball, and ballpoint.

"What, no mammo nose ring or mammo belly ring?" I
asked.

Amy laughed. "We'll see. Let's give it a year."

"No, seriously," I said. "Bottom line."

"Bottom line what?"

"Bottom line—how much time will I be able to take off
from work if the deal goes through?"

She took her glasses off and pushed her pads away, and I
nervously felt the need to clarify my question.

"How much time will I be able to take off from work if I
decide to—"

"Have a baby?"

It was practically July already, and the Labor Day decision
deadline was rapidly approaching.

"Let's put it this way," Amy said, a smile slowly spreading
across her face. "If this deal goes through—*when* this deal
goes through—you'll probably be able to quit your job for
good. Your friend Renee, as designer, should be happy with
her cut of the royalties. She could probably quit her job,
too."

"She'd never quit her job," I said. "No matter how much
money she had, she'd always work. It's what she loves to do
most in the world."

We beamed at each other, then clinked our glasses together to toast my good fortune.

"So you've been awfully quiet lately," I said.

"How do you mean?"

"I mean about everything. About dating. About the baby decision now. The last two months have been so crazy because of Karen's shower and the gift and the deal, that I feel like I have no idea where you are with things."

She sipped her wine and shifted in the big leather chair. The air conditioning made the room feel almost cold, but compared with the heat and humidity outside, it was actually a relief. She pulled a little black cardigan sweater out of her bag and threw it around her shoulders.

"Where I am with things," she said. "That's a good question. Since I think I'm in a different place now than I was before."

I waited for her to continue.

"I've met someone."

I raised an eyebrow. *"Really."*

"Someone who's good to me. Who's good for me."

"Good to you and for you? Well, this is a new concept for us."

"I know. Positivity. In its purest form."

"How long has this been going on?"

"A couple of weeks at least. Maybe a month, I guess."

Again I raised an eyebrow.

"I've been wanting to tell you, but I didn't want to do it on the phone."

"So tell me already," I said eagerly, pretending not to care that she'd kept me in the dark this long. "Who is he?"

"His name is Barry. Barry Weller."

"What does he do?"

"Real estate lawyer. Like me."

"And how'd you meet?"

"On a blind date."

"You're kidding."

"Nope. After three hundred total losers, I finally got lucky."

"So is he—"

"Cute? No. Not particularly."

"Smart?"

"Very smart."

"And you get along?"

She nodded. Then she paused, as if she'd had this conversation with herself many times before and was getting pretty good at answering her own most difficult questions.

"He's not the most exciting person in the world. But he's nice. And he adores me. And he wants to get married and have children. And that's, well, as you know, that's what I want, too."

"You mean you might actually *marry* him?" I could hardly believe that Amy had met someone so potentially significant and I was only finding out about it now.

She shrugged.

"Are you in love with him?"

"I don't know yet. He's in love with me, though. And I suppose six months from now, if I seem in the least bit interested, which I probably will be, he'll probably start talking seriously about the future."

I wanted to say something then about settling—about why she was settling for someone she clearly felt no passion for when she was still, relatively, so young. But she knew what she was doing, it seemed; she'd clearly thought about her life long and hard these months after Will. Who was I to presume to tell her what was settling and what wasn't?

"You're disappointed in me," she said.

"I'm not. I'm really not."

"You think I'm settling."

She was putting me on the spot, and we both knew it.

"I probably am," she said, letting me off the hook without

offering any further explanation or excuse, and I was relieved.

In the eight months since we'd met again, we'd covered an awful lot of ground, she and I. We were coming through our emotional tunnels now—she first, and me soon to follow—and in the near future there would be enough harsh light to judge our decisions. The last thing either of us needed was to be judged harshly by each other.

"I want you to be happy," I said finally. "And if Barry can offer you the kind of life that will make you happy, then I'm all for it."

She looked at me skeptically.

"I *am.*"

And I would be, in a week, or two, or three, once I'd had time to get used to it all. In minutes, though, I realized the practical ramifications of her news.

"So does this mean what I think it means?" I said.

She looked at me sheepishly and nodded.

"No two-for-one sperm-bank pregnancies, I guess, huh?"

"I'm sorry," she said.

"Me, too." And I was. "So I guess I'm on my own—*really* on my own in this. No boyfriend. No best friend. Just me and my pregnancy books and my sample donor profile and one month left to decide. That's a sad sorry state of affairs, isn't it?"

"What if you can't decide by then?"

"I'm not expecting any trouble in that regard, but if I run into any, I'll give myself an extension. A few weeks. A few months. Another year if I have to. However long it takes before I'm sure—completely sure—about my decision."

She finished her drink, too. "Any word from—?"

"Malcolm? No. Nothing."

Not for almost three months.

"What's the point, I guess, right?" she said. "I mean, at

least he's had the grace to leave you alone and let you get on with your life."

"I suppose."

"Of course, it would have been nice if he'd come crawling back," she added. "Just like Will didn't. But getting back to the pregnancy question," she said, glancing back over at her pad of paper. "I mean, now that money's not going to be a problem, it's easier to decide. Isn't it?"

No.

It wasn't easier.

In fact, it was even harder.

Now that the last major obstacle had been removed, I had no more excuses left.

17

. . .

BY AUGUST 1 the contract for the deal with Tiffany had been finalized and signed by all concerned parties, and a large initial on-signing payment—more than an equivalent year's salary—was due to me by early October. Amy and Ward had gone over the contract carefully, changing things that Amy would then try to explain to me—the most important one being that my future contractual payout amounts were not contingent upon sales of the necklace. This meant that if the line sold badly, I would still receive the monies they had promised me, and if the line sold well, I would receive additional monies, once Tiffany had earned back the initial outlay that they had paid me.

"If I'd known this was going to be such a success," Renee said when I went over her part of the contract, "I wouldn't have been so hard on you when you first tried to explain mammo to me. Even though you deserved it, since nothing you said that day made any sense."

Which was, I figured, her way of saying thank you.

Shortly after the paperwork was finalized, I started to give serious thought to taking time off from work. I needed some time and space to think—to think as clearly and as deeply as I could in order to make my final decision. I had never *not* had a job, and I wondered if not having a place to go to every day or people to talk to would depress me. But I was too superstitious to quit outright before I'd received any money, so I decided I'd first ask Karen for a six-month leave of absence and go from there.

She was still on maternity leave, surprisingly enough, since we all thought she'd have come back a week after her epi-siotomy stitches came out, but it seemed that carrying around such a massive fetus for all that time while working seven days a week had taken its toll even on her. For the first time since I'd known Karen—and probably since anyone had known her—she was exhausted, and doctor's orders had precluded her from returning to work for another month at least.

"Since the mountain can't come to the office, the office is going to have to come to the mountain," Gail said, answering Karen's home phone during that first week. As Simon, who would be working from Karen's for the rest of the month, explained it to those of us in the office, all of the KLNY depart-ment heads would make a pilgrimage to Karen's apartment on Monday mornings for a weekly meeting. An additional assistant would be hired for Karen, who would messenger a pouch to her at the beginning and end of every day so that business could proceed apace. It was via this pouch that I sent my written request for a leave of absence to Karen, and it was from this pouch that her approval came back to me—with something very unexpected. "O.K." was written and circled with her trademark red grease pencil, but instead of her usual initials, she had signed her memo this way: "Mammo Karen."

IN THE MIDDLE of September, I heard from Simon that Arlene Schiffler had given birth to a seven-pound eight-ounce baby girl—via cesarean—and had, in the time since I'd seen her at Karen's shower in May, gained sixty pounds.

Sixty pounds.

Somehow, though, she did manage to have a piece about her delivery come out almost immediately in *Glamour*—the ninth and final month's entry of her "Nine Months" series. And it seemed to Amy and me, when we read it aloud to each other one night over the phone, screaming and howling at how disgustingly self-involved she was, that she must have written two versions—*vaginal delivery* and *cesarean delivery*—well before the actual event and phoned in the correct version from the hospital.

Had I not been so tired of her columns and so tired of baby-gift buying—the Karen extravaganza having been only the most prominent baby gift in a year of constant baby-gift giving—I might have sent her something. But I was preparing to take a much-needed break from the business of professional falseness, and I was longing to stop doing things I didn't want to do.

And besides, I was getting ready to go up to Maine to be with my sister before her due date, and I had a lot on my mind.

I had to think of a nickname for the baby.

Something a little more original than Co-Pickle, or Vice-Pickle.

LYNN GAVE BIRTH to an eight-pound three-ounce baby boy, David Samuel—via cesarean, again—at nine o'clock on the morning of July 10th. When her contractions started in the middle of the night, she and Paul went to the hospital at four-thirty, and my parents, who had come to Maine early in anticipation of the birth, met them there shortly afterward, leaving me alone with Nicole.

She and I were up having our waffles by the time they called to tell us the news. And when I hung up, I told Nicole to finish eating because we had a special day ahead of us.

"Remember Mum-Mum and Daddy told you that Mum-Mum's in the hospital even though she's not sick?" It was bright and chilly that early Tuesday morning, and the breeze rattled the window jambs in the breakfast nook as we ate.

Nicole seemed unusually quiet as she dipped a bite-size waffle cube into the little puddle of syrup on the side of her plate. "Uh-huh."

"Well, when we go to visit her in a little while, she's going to have a surprise for you."

Lynn and Paul had been preparing her for a new baby brother for months now. "I know what it is." She stuck her fingers in her mouth and whispered as if she were suddenly shy.

I knelt down in front of her to button up her little green sweater. "And what is it?"

"It's Baby Boy."

"And do you know what Baby Boy's name is?"

"It's David Samuel."

I gave her a hug and held her close to me.

"Auntie LaLa?"

"Yes, sweetheart?"

"How long is Baby Boy going to stay here for?"

I couldn't help but laugh. My mother had always told us how Lynn had asked the same question about me when I was born.

"He's going to stay forever."

"What's forever?"

"Forever's a long, long time."

"Are you staying forever?"

I took her little hand and brought it up to my mouth and

kissed it. I could feel the back of my throat tighten, and I knew I'd have trouble getting the words out. "No. I'm not staying forever."

"How long are you staying for, then?"

"For a week. So I can help Mum-Mum with the new baby."

"I wish you could stay longer."

"I know. Me, too."

"Then you could play with me. And sleep in my bed with me."

"I know. I love playing with you and sleeping in your bed with you."

"Because you know what?" She put her hands on my face lightly, as if she wanted to know what the skin felt like, and when she looked me in the eyes, I felt my throat seize up again. This was my Pickle, the little girl I loved more than life itself, and we would always be friends. No matter how old she got.

"What?"

"When you go away, I miss you a lot and a lot, and really bad."

"And when I go away, I miss you a lot and a lot, and really bad, too." I gave her another hug and then patted on her Pull-Up. "Come," I said on the way to the car, "Mammo's waiting."

THE MINUTE I laid eyes on David that day, I knew that I was going to be as crazy about him as I'd been about Nicole. Holding him, draping him over my shoulder as I'd done with my niece four years ago, made my heart hurt, and I relished the infant smell of his little head and the feel of his tiny new cotton one-piece pajamas under my palm. Dark haired with big black eyes, he looked to me exactly like Lynn.

"You think?" she said, still groggy from the painkillers. Paul had taken Nicole to the cafeteria, so it was just the three of us in Lynn's quiet, dark hospital room. I was sitting on the edge of her bed. "Everybody keeps saying he looks just like Paul."

"Well, he does. But he's got—"

"My eye thing?" She pushed the sides of her eyes down. "My stupid droopy eyes?"

"No," I said, smiling. "He's got your fat thing. The sixteen double chins. And twenty rolls of stomach flab."

She tried to laugh without moving so she wouldn't pull on her cesarean stitches.

"I was kidding, you know."

"I know. But don't make me laugh. It hurts."

"Okay."

We both looked at David sleeping on Lynn's chest.

"He's amazing," I said. "Truly amazing."

"Isn't he?"

At that moment I could think of nothing more wonderful than him. Nothing. Tears came into my eyes. Tears came into her eyes, too, and she took my hand.

"Are you going to do it?"

"I'm not sure yet. I go around and around, thinking about it and thinking about it." I reached for a tissue and wiped my nose.

"It's a big decision."

"It's a huge decision."

"Is Malcolm a possibility?"

"No. Not anymore. Not for a while now."

"I'm sorry."

"It's okay."

She squeezed my hand. "Well, what about other—?"

"Alternatives? I'm looking into them."

"Do it," she said suddenly.

I turned to face her.

"Just do it. You'll never be sorry."

"You sound so sure."

"I am sure."

"But why?"

"How," she said, cupping the back of the baby's head in her hand, "could you ever regret this?"

I STAYED THE following week, helping out with meals and laundry and errands and with anything else that needed to be done. This was, basically, everything, since when Lynn came home from the hospital, all she could do was lie around trying not to aggravate the pain from her cesarean scar and breast-feeding twenty-four hours a day. My main job and, needless to say, my favorite job, was taking care of the Pickle. The usual nonstop marathon of *Barney*-watching and story-reading ensued, as did the occasional "no"- induced tantrums, which seemed at an all-time high this visit.

Which was understandable.

It would take some time to adjust to the fact that there was a new little Monkey in the house.

ON MY NEXT visit, during the long Labor Day weekend, Nicole was in love with her little brother, nose-kissing him at every opportunity.

On the Tuesday afternoon before I returned to New York, I took a walk along the beach at Widow's Cove. It was a few miles from my sister's house, so I drove there and parked the Jeep in the lot, which was empty now that the season was officially over.

The air was clear and breezy and almost chilly as I walked

barefoot at the water's edge. Overnight, it seemed, the season had changed. In New England, Labor Day meant the end of summer, and without a moment's hesitation, the air and the light looked different. This day could no sooner have been mistaken for a day in early June than it could have been mistaken for a day in late February—and I envied nature its absoluteness, its clarity.

It was after six when I went back to the parking lot. I unlocked the car and sat behind the steering wheel, keeping my legs outside the door so I could brush the sand off my feet and put my shoes back on. The soft clang of distant buoys and the sharp squawks of seagulls flying overhead had a sadness to them, and sitting there, listening to the sounds of summer disappearing, I suddenly felt completely and utterly alone, and I knew it with a certainty I had never known before. I felt it in my bones, and in every cell of my body, and to the very core of my being, and in the flash of an instant— in a flash of vision and insight and time fast-forwarding itself inside my eyes—I saw that I could be alone like that forever, and I knew, at that moment, that I could not bear it.

And that I did not have to bear it.

I could have my own child—my own Pickle, my own Monkey.

I could be somebody's mammo.

Finally, I knew what I wanted to do.

THE
THIRD
TRIMESTER

18

. . .

RESOLVING TO HAVE a baby and going about actually having one as a single woman were two very different things. I realized this once my leave had started, while I paced around my apartment and watched *Sesame Street* and *Barney.*

I wanted to call Amy for guidance, but she had taken a week off to go leaf-peeping with Barry in Vermont, and besides, she had gotten off the sperm-bank-baby path a while ago. So I called Renee at work instead.

"You said we had a varied and multilayered friendship, so now's your chance to prove it to me."

"I'm *not* joining a dating service," she said, which is what she always said when I suggested we try to think of ways to improve our antisocial social lives.

"That wasn't what I was going to ask you."

"Then what?"

"I thought, since you're so good at designing clothes for men, that you'd be the perfect person to help me pick one out."

"From where?"
"A sperm-bank catalog."

I'D ALREADY DONE a fair amount of preliminary research, which would spare Renee any unnecessary boredom ("I don't want to sit there while you weed through the entire world of sperm"), so I knew that while you could browse the donor profiles on the computer once you'd registered, you needed to be under the care of a doctor, who would order the sperm for you.

I'd also found out that at my sperm bank of choice—Cryogenesis—all donors undergo a psychological evaluation using the Minnesota Multiphasic Personality Inventory and are screened repeatedly by licensed psychotherapists.

And that the average age of their donors was 29.3 years.

And that less than five percent of the men who apply to become part of the Semen Donor Program are accepted.

And that since the first successful artificial insemination with frozen human semen was achieved in 1953, more than 200,000 births had been reported using cryopreserved human semen, with another 30,000 births taking place annually.

And that you can purchase extra vials of a particular donor's sperm to keep in reserve in case you want to have several children by the same donor.

And that the cost of the sperm-purchasing process will run somewhere in the vicinity of $1,600 for frozen semen specimens and around $2,400 for fresh semen specimens—not including "assisted reproduction procedures," which could run anywhere from $350 to $600 with each insemination attempt, depending on your medical insurance.

Logging on to Cryogenesis that night—for real this time—I pulled up the Semen Donor Catalog, which provided a complete list of all active donors and a detailed view of their physical characteristics as well as their maternal and paternal ancestry, education/occupations, and special interests. Then, once I had narrowed down the selection of possible candidates, I could order a five-page detailed dossier (Data Assisted Donor Selection, also known by its official acronym as DADS, *ha ha!*) on each for fifteen dollars a pop. I could even get a Photo Assisted Donor Selection (*PADS?*), which is where you send a photo of the person you want your child to resemble, and the staff ranks the resemblance of the donors you've selected to make the best match.

I entered my password ("Big Bird") and selected the browsing menu. Instantly an array of questions appeared— *preferred eye color, hair color, skin color, height, religion*—presumably to help me start choosing from donors who looked something like me and nothing like Danny Bonaducci. I entered brown, brown, Caucasian, and tall and left the preferred religion blank, since at this point whether or not the donor was Jewish seemed irrelevant, not to mention ridiculous, though I was sure my parents would have disagreed. In seconds 172 profiles matching those physical preferences were available for browsing.

And so I started.

I eliminated the first ten profiles right off the bat, the way a trial lawyer eliminates potential jurors for probable cause—uninteresting professions-to-be (business major); excessive height (six foot six).

By the end of the week, I'd narrowed it down to a total of seven donors who looked promising, then ordered the DADS. The extended profiles with photos arrived a few days later by Federal Express, and keeping her word, Renee came over to help me make my final selections.

"I'm sweating like a pig," she said, walking into my apartment for the first time and looking around as if, given the chance, she'd change every single thing in it. It was Indian summer, and she looked tormented in her signature black clothing. "Where's your air conditioner?"

I pointed to it, and she went over and turned it up all the way.

"Can I get you something? Water? Juice? Diet Coke?"

She followed me into the kitchen, pushed me toward the refrigerator, and took a slim clear bottle out of her big black bag. "Just get me a glass of ice. I brought my own beverage."

Vodka.

And so it began.

File 1:

"This one looks like a nonfag," she said once we'd settled onto the floor of the now-freezing-cold living room. She threw the file she'd picked into the preliminary keep pile.

File 2:

"Fag."

Discard pile.

File 3:

"Wacko."

Discard.

File 4:

"Nonfag."

Keep.

Files 5 and 6:

"Wacko. Fag. Ugly. Boring."

Discard.

Discard.

File 7:

"Okay, wait." She made the face a sixteen-year-old boy would make if he thought a girl was hot.

"What?" I said, putting down the folder I was looking through. "Another nonfag?"

She nodded, mesmerized, pointing at the photograph. "He's adorable."

I looked over her shoulder. Brown hair, brown eyes, good teeth, strong jaw, no facial hair. "Not bad."

"Not *bad*? What are you, a fucking dead person? He's the cutest guy I've seen in about ten years." She scanned down to the bottom of the page and flipped to the next one. "And he's studying to be an *architect*."

"He's not my future husband, Renee. He's a *sperm donor*. Remember?"

She sat back in her chair and looked slightly deflated. "I know. But I can't help it."

"Help what?"

"I'm a romantic. I want you to pick out the best guy so you can have the best kid."

I put my folder down and smiled at her. *"You're a romantic?"* She flinched.

"Mrs. He's-a-Wacko-He's-a-Fag has a little bit of hope left in there?" I reached over and tried to poke her in the ribs near her heart, but she smacked my hand away. Only Renee would be perverse enough to feel sentimental and romantic while sitting around looking at sperm donor profiles.

She gave me the finger.

"Asswipe," she said under her breath.

"Asswipe," I replied.

By the time the evening had ended, she'd helped me narrow my selection down to two potential donors. Being a romantic, too, I went to sleep that night with visions of Nicole and David behind my eyes.

THE FOLLOWING WEEK I called my gynecologist for a referral. Since I was over thirty-five, she referred me to a fertility specialist: Dr. Singh Vishnu, on Park Avenue and Eighty-first Street. And because she liked me, she got them to squeeze me in the next week. I could hardly wait. My

Tuesday appointment finally came, and before I knew it, I was in a cab, then in the waiting room, then ushered from the waiting room into the doctor's office as he came rushing in behind me from an examination room next door.

"I am Dr. Vishnu," he said, reaching out to shake my hand before he sat down behind his desk. "And you are"—he glanced at my file, which he'd brought with him—"Ms. Franck."

"Ellen."

He nodded. "Ellen." He was a small balding man with gigantic glasses, and as he scanned my file, his giant leather chair dwarfed him in the same way that Karen's giant chair dwarfed her. "Tell me, Ms.—Ellen—why you have come."

Had he not seemed so genuinely curious and had I not been so nervous, I might have been glib, or tried to be funny, or shifted into excessive self-deprecation. But there was something—a warmth, a kindness—in his eyes and in his voice that melted me, and so I just said this:

"I want to have a baby."

Suddenly the enormity of what I was doing—sitting in a fertility doctor's office and starting the huge grinding wheels of procreation in motion—hit me, and I panicked.

"I think I want to have a baby," I stammered. "I mean, I know I want to have one. I'm just not sure I want to do it today."

He grinned. "Yes, well. That is a good thing, as I am com-*plete*ly booked today."

We both laughed, and I relaxed a bit.

"What I meant was, I'm not sure I'm ready to do it immediately. But I want to get started on the process."

He nodded and looked back at my file. "You are—not married, and not with a partner?"

"Correct." I was tempted to clarify the fact that I was not

a lesbian—wasn't that the obvious stereotype?—but since it didn't matter, I let it go.

"And you have decided on artificial insemination by a donor of known or unknown origin?"

"I'm not sure what you mean."

"A donor of known origin would be a friend, or an acquaintance, or someone with whom you've made an arrangement to become pregnant. A donor of unknown origin would be, most simply, an anonymous sperm donor."

"Oh. Of course," I said. "Unknown, then."

"Tell me. You are familiar with this process? The steps involved before artificial insemination can take place?"

Ever the good student, I nodded: I'd done my homework.

"I'm down to two potential sperm donors."

"*Very* good. Now let me explain. We will examine you to rule out any problems regarding fertility. If there are problems, of course, we will advise a course of treatment and proceed accordingly. This is to prevent you from wasting time and money on inseminations if you are not able to conceive."

Neither Lynn nor my mother had had any trouble conceiving, so I looked at him expectantly to tell me the rest.

"After that you will discuss with a counselor here your decision to have a child independently—psychological considerations and also practical considerations: employment, financial planning, medical insurance, day care. Once you have gone through these steps and everything is in order, we can then approach the final stage of insemination."

I let out a deep breath, then looked at an arrangement of family photographs on the credenza behind him. They were of his wife and his children—two sons and a daughter who were, judging from the latest snapshots, almost grown.

"Do you have any questions for me? Something you would like to discuss that I can help you with?"

I wanted to ask him a thousand questions—*Should I wait? Will I ever meet anyone? Will I ever be happy?*—but all I could do was shrug.

"What do you think I should do?" I whispered.

He smiled sympathetically.

"I mean, if I were your daughter—if she were in my position, what would you tell her to do? Would you tell her to do it now, or would you tell her to wait?"

"Technically at thirty-five—almost thirty-six—you are by no means at the end of your fertility cycle, though problems and complications with fertility do increase with time."

I wanted him to continue, I wanted him to tell me what to do, for someone older and wiser to tell me that no matter what I decided, it would all be okay—but I knew he couldn't do that. No one could. And that was life, plain and simple.

"I am advising only that when you are certain of your decision, you act sooner rather than later."

Which is what I did.

I SET UP a schedule of examination and follow-up appointments with Dr. Vishnu's secretary over the coming weeks. During this time, I met with a reproductive counselor and discussed the practical and financial considerations of my decision.

Did I have a source of income and a suitable place to live? Yes.

Did I plan on returning to work immediately after the baby was born? If so, what childcare arrangements would I make?

No, I did not plan on going back to work right away. The voluntary six-month leave I was currently on would either be extended another six months or would become permanent, so it would be me taking care of the baby.

Did my family and friends approve of what I was doing?

Pause.

Did my family and friends know what I was doing?

Not yet.

Because . . . ?

Because . . . I didn't think it made sense to tell them anything until there was something to tell them.

So when and if I became pregnant . . . ?

So when and if I became pregnant, I would happily spread the news.

Did I know yet what I would tell my child about the circumstances of their conception and birth?

No, I did not.

Did I feel confident that in four or five years—or whenever the time came—I could come up with a viable explanation?

Yes.

Was I comfortable with what I was doing—that is, did I feel completely sure I was making the right decision to become pregnant by the sperm of an unknown donor?

Yes. Would it have been my first choice, however? No.

All that was left to do now was to come to a final decision about the sperm donor.

A new feeling of resolve had set in by then, gradually calming all the different emotions that were roiling around in my head. Once in a while I'd think about the office— how Karen's spring line was being put together now without me; what pandemonium had taken place there just before "Fashion Week" last month—but I felt very removed from that world. It was hard to believe that over a year had passed since I'd first run into Amy, and it was hard to believe the magnitude of the changes that had occurred since then. I'd broken up with Malcolm; both Lynn and Karen had each had her second child; I'd created mammo, and would probably never have to work again.

By Thanksgiving I'd decided on the architect-to-be. I was ready to take the final step without hesitation or ambivalence.

The order for the sperm was placed through Dr. Vishnu's office.

And at the precise moment of my next ovulation cycle, on a clear cold early December morning, I raced up to Eighty-first Street and Park Avenue.

As fast as the legs of my gum-ball machine full of eggs would carry me.

EPILOGUE

19

. . .

ASIDE FROM THE morning sickness, and the weight gain, and the swollen hands and feet, and the fact that I can't stay up past nine anymore, and the early-morning insomnia, and the occasional panic attacks I get when I think about the amniocentesis I'll have to have and when I wonder about the huge leap of faith I've made—I'm having a relatively easy first trimester.

Believe it or not, my test was positive after only one insemination. This surprised me and made me revise a few aspects of my new nine-month plan, since I'd padded it with several extra months of insemination attempts. Dr. Vishnu was surprised, too—so surprised, in fact, that when he called to tell me the news, he went on and on about how getting pregnant at my age on the first round of assisted-pregnancy techniques was highly unlikely. I assumed he was paying me a compliment, or at least trying to, by making me feel good about the apparent viability of the few old eggs I'd had left. But even if he was simply being scientific, the speed and ease with which it had happened made the whole thing seem destined.

I waited awhile to tell my parents—my mother, actually—until the week between Christmas and New Year's, when we all descended on my sister in Maine. I dreaded taking both of them on at once, and since I knew that my father was ultimately the easier of the two to tell, I decided to get the worst over with first. One afternoon when my father was napping, I got my mother alone in the kitchen while she was making a salad. It was dusk then, and the house was unusually quiet.

"I have something to tell you," I said.

She looked up at me from the cutting board with her *Who died?* face. "What's the matter?"

"Nothing's the matter."

"You're not sick, then."

"No. I'm not sick." I edged a step or two closer to her along the counter. And then I told her.

Everything.

My obsession with Nicole and Amy's obsession with Isabel. Lynn and Karen's pregnancies. Arlene Schiffler's column and the deadline it inspired. Internet sperm bank-browsing. My breakup with Malcolm. Walking along the beach after David's birth. My decision to become a single mother by choice and Amy's decision not to. The sperm donor selection. Dr. Vishnu and the insemination. The day I got the phone call that it took.

And as I talked I watched her face fall. And fall. And fall some more.

Long ago, if I'd ever thought about what it would be like to tell my mother I was pregnant, I probably would have envisioned myself in a pretty kitchen in a pretty house in a pretty suburb, my husband in the next room, a wedding ring on my finger, and her face: happy, excited, relieved. I'm sure she had imagined a scenario like this, too, which was why she was rendered completely speechless. For a moment, anyway.

"I don't know what to say," she eventually managed. "I'm in shock."

I leaned against the counter and crossed my arms in front of me. I'd expected this reaction. It was always about her, it seemed; always about how things affected her. She had never been able to hear anything Lynn and I ever said without taking it personally.

The silence between us was thick with disappointment and disapproval. "Okay . . ." I said. Meaning: *And what else?*

She threw her hands up melodramatically. "When is this . . . when are you due?"

"September."

"And you're prepared for this? For all the responsibilities and problems that come with having a baby?"

"Joy comes with it, too," I said. But suddenly I could feel the bottom start to fall out of my insides and the doubt rushing in like air after a vacuum.

She conceded the point with some reluctance. "And the joy."

"As prepared as anyone ever is, I think."

"Because you've taken on a huge commitment. That's a lot for one person to cope with. Alone."

I winced at the word, but I was determined not to let her pessimism infect me, defeat me, the way it had so many times before.

"Look, I know my life hasn't always turned out the way you expected," I said slowly, feeling my way around the words inside my head. "That I haven't turned out the way you expected."

"And what way is that?"

"Normal. Like all your friends' children. You know, living nearby. Married. Kids." I answered her without a second's hesitation, and it surprised me. And saddened me, since I realized that one of the things I still wanted most was for my mother to approve of me, to like me. "My life hasn't turned out the way *I* expected it to either. I mean, I never, in a million years, expected to make a decision like this. To have to make a decision like this. But then again, I feel lucky. Because it's a decision I could make: I'm going to be able to have a baby after all."

"A*lone?*" she repeated.

"Yes," I said. "Alone." I stared her down but felt increasingly guilty as I watched her eyes fill up with tears, and it was only then as she reached for a dish towel to wipe them away that I realized she was afraid for me. We were not a particularly fearless lot, our family; did not often believe in a benevolent future, though we did have our rare moments of hopefulness. And this, as it turned out, would be one of them.

"I may not always be alone."

She shrugged. *True.*

"And besides: I'm *not* alone. I have a few really good friends. And I have Lynn. She'll help me."

"Of course she will." She turned away to wash her hands at the sink, but I could tell from the way she tried to hide her face from me that I'd hurt her feelings without meaning to.

"And maybe, if you feel you want to, *you* could help me."

She turned back around. "You want my help?"

"Of course I do. Why wouldn't I?"

"I'm just surprised, that's all. I can't remember the last time you asked for it."

I thought a minute. I couldn't either.

She wiped her eyes again, then put the towel down, and then she hugged me. And in that one moment, in that one familiar instant of standing in the kitchen by the sink with my mother, each of us trying to understand the other and once, in a blue moon, succeeding, I knew the flood of doubt had been pushed back. Maybe she had never been able to say the right thing at the right time, but I had always believed

that in the end, my mother would stand by me. And knowing that she'd be there to teach me how to feed and bathe
and diaper a baby, that she'd be there to teach me everything
she knew about being a mother—however imperfect I may
have thought her mothering skills were (was there a daughter on earth who *didn't* think her mother's mothering skills
were imperfect?)—I felt less alone than I had in a very long
time.

AUGUST 30 WAS my due date, at least by Dr. Vishnu's
calculations.

I'd told Lynn, of course, the week before, when I'd gotten
there ahead of everyone else. She and I had just exchanged
presents—I gave her a mammo necklace of course (in white
gold), and she gave me a silver locket, inside of which was a
teeny-tiny photograph of the Pickle and the Monkey, who
looked very distinguished for all of his four months. When I
broke the news, she started tiptoeing excitedly around the
house, giving me her favorite early-stage sweatpants and
pulling whatever pregnancy books I didn't already have off
the shelves. Which I brought home and added to my
already-extensive collection.

I've gone back to those books, and except for the husband
stuff, they make sense. Every night I get into bed and read
one, and then I even fill out a diary page in the *What to
Expect When You're Expecting* "Daily Pregnancy Journal" that
Amy gave me a few days after I told her. She's given me a
whole bunch of other things too since, I suspect, she still
feels a little guilty for not getting pregnant, too—like a black
Lycra four-piece essential leggings-skirt-tunic-dress
Pregnancy Survival Kit and two stuffed dolls: one Barney
and one Big Bird, for old times' sake.

A month ago, right after New Year's, she and Barry got

engaged, and while I wasn't beside myself with joy, I tried to be, and I think I was almost convincing. At least, I hope I was. He really was nice, and he was clearly head over heels in love with her. I even offered to help her go looking for a wedding dress once my all-day morning sickness subsides, but she reminded me that she still has her old one. Good thing she held on to it.

A few weeks ago I started looking at larger apartments and cribs and strollers and changing tables and nursery wallpaper and color schemes, but I became completely overwhelmed. I asked Renee if she would make all these decisions for me so I could just go about the business of being pregnant without any additional stress, but she said since I'm going to *have* a baby I better stop *being* a baby and do it myself, and that she has enough to do preparing to be my birth coach.

I guess she's just saving all her nurturing skills and moral support for the delivery room.

Karen is back at work now. I called her recently to tell her my good news, though I assumed she'd already heard it from Simon. While she wasn't about to start trading pregnancy war-stories with me or offering to share baby clothes, she did say that if I ever needed anything—*anything*—she would always be there to help me, and I believed her. Simon calls once in a while with gossip and news from the office, and last week I recognized his handiwork when I saw an item in the *New York Observer* with the boldfaced subhead "Karen Skipps a Meal at the Grill Room."

Arlene Schiffler, of course, has a new column, "The First Year of Motherhood"—and when I need a good laugh or after I've had a good cry because I'm afraid of doing everything I have to do alone, I'll buy the latest issue of *Glamour* or reread a grotesque diary entry from an earlier month to Amy over the phone until the panic and terror and fear of the unknown subsides. Comfort seems to come from the oddest places these days, but when it does, I'm usually far too grateful to question it.

Or already asleep.

MALCOLM CALLED ONE night, out of the blue, during the second week of February. I'd been standing in the middle of the living room wondering if there was some other configuration of furniture that would miraculously provide enough extra space for a nursery so I wouldn't have to move, when the phone rang. Ten months had passed since we'd spoken, and while I used to occasionally rehearse a script should he ever call again, when I finally did hear him asking me how I was, I had no idea what to say.

We made small talk for a few minutes—I told him I was on leave, and he told me he was teaching at Columbia now instead of the New School. Then he told me that he'd thought a lot about me and our relationship over the months we'd been apart, and asked if we could get together and talk. And because by this point I thought seeing him and talking to him couldn't do me any harm and could only do me some good—closure and setting things right between us and all that other therapy-speak stuff—I agreed to meet him for a drink at the Cedar Tavern in an hour.

It took me almost that long to figure out what to wear, since everything I owned was already a little tight and would only make me look fat, though not necessarily fat and pregnant. But I quickly realized that it didn't matter what I wore, so I ripped into the Pregnancy Survival Kit and put on the leggings and tunic. Then I grabbed my keys and my coat and quickly walked the few blocks to meet him.

He was already there when I came in from the cold—sitting in a booth, for once—and when he saw me come in, he waved, then stood up as I approached the table. We looked at each other awkwardly before he reached behind me to help me off with my coat. He put his arms around me and hugged me quickly but tightly.

He went to order me a drink from the bartender and a minute or two later returned with my cranberry juice.

"It's good to see you," he said.

"It's good to see you, too." Sitting with him again was as easy as it had always been, and for a moment it felt as if those ten long months hadn't passed at all. But I was afraid of enjoying it too much. He might not call again for another ten months.

"You look good. You look—"

I smiled. "Fat?"

"No. You just look good."

"I do?"

He nodded.

"Thanks." Malcolm didn't often hand out compliments, so when he did, they meant a lot—especially given our last conversation and my current vulnerable state of mind. "You look very—"

"Fat?" he said, imitating me.

I laughed. "No. *Fit.*"

"I started running again."

"I didn't know you used to run."

"I did. A lot. Marathons, even."

"Really."

"It's one of the few small but significant changes I've made in my life recently. I sold my apartment. And I'm buying a place downtown. On Fifth Avenue and Tenth Street. Right near you, actually," he added.

"Right near me."

"I'm still going to have the long commute that I had

before, only now it'll be in reverse. But I thought it was time for a change."

"Well, that's quite a change—uptown to downtown." I knew that wasn't the kind of change he'd meant, but I was stalling for time. I wasn't sure if I wanted to open that particular can of worms before he did.

"I also started writing—a little."

"That's great," I said. "I'm happy for you." I had never heard him say anything about his writing, and knowing how much it had meant to him once, I was moved now to hear he was inching back toward it.

He shrugged. "It's not great yet. But at least I'm doing it."

"That's a pretty big 'at least.' "

He nodded. "What about you?" he said.

Me?

"I read about your success with the necklace. That's terrific."

"Thanks."

"So now that you're on leave—now that you don't have to do a job you hate for a while—have you decided what to do next?"

"Kind of. I'm still in the planning stages, though."

"Listen," he said, "I asked you to meet me here because I wanted you to know that I thought about what you said that night, the last time we were here. I thought about it a lot. And you were right."

"Right about what?"

"About everything." He shifted in his seat. "I was frozen. Completely frozen. I wasn't ready to"—he looked up at the ceiling as if he might find a way to say what he wanted to say—"I wasn't ready for you. But now I am."

I was completely shocked to hear him say that. Dumbstruck, in fact. "Oh," I said flatly.

He took a sip from his drink, then rubbed his hand dry. "I have no idea where you are with things. If you're happier without me. If you've met someone else. For all I know, you could be engaged by now."

"I'm not engaged."

I was *pregnant,* but I was not engaged.

He ran his hands along the edge of the table. "I want to try again. I want—I want to be with you."

I sat back against the hard wood of the booth and put my hands in my lap. I'd imagined this scenario a thousand times—him saying these exact words, wanting me back—but now that it was actually happening, I felt numb.

"I know that a lot didn't work between us, but I'm getting better, I think. I'm seeing someone now, a therapist, and he's good. I've got a long way to go, but I feel—I feel more like myself than I have in a long time."

"I can tell," I said. "You seem—well, you seem more at peace with yourself."

He looked at me. "But?"

I smiled and shrugged. "But—a lot of things."

"Like what?"

"Like—things are different now. I'm different now."

"Are you involved with someone?"

"No."

"Then how are things different?"

I knew I had to tell him the truth. And I wanted to tell him. He had, after all, had a great deal to do with my decision.

"I'm pregnant."

His mouth dropped open. "How far along are you?"

"Eleven weeks."

"Eleven weeks," he repeated. "Was it—was it an accident?"

"No. It wasn't. It was planned."

He swallowed hard. "With someone you knew?"

"No. I can't say I've ever met anyone at the Cryogenesis International Sperm Bank."

He sat back against the hard wood of the booth now, too, and after what seemed like forever, he smiled. "Jesus, that's brave."

"Brave? I didn't do it because I was brave. I did it because I was terrified. Terrified of what I'd miss if I didn't do it."

"Are you still terrified?"

"Sometimes. Sometimes, in the middle of the night, when I think about the enormity of what I've done and whether things will turn out okay, yes, I feel terrified."

"Don't be."

I laughed. "Easy for you to say."

"No, it isn't."

Of course it wasn't. "I'm sorry. I didn't mean to be glib." Somehow there seemed to be an opening, so I decided to take it. "When your wife was pregnant," I started slowly, "with Benjamin, were you scared?"

He thought a minute. "No. I wasn't scared. I was excited. I was happy. I felt like my life was finally starting." He disappeared from behind his eyes for a few seconds, and in that brief time it seemed he went somewhere very far away. When he came back and looked at me, I saw a film of tears. He had indeed come far since we'd been apart. "The fear will pass," he said softly. "It will pass."

"It will?" I covered my eyes with my palms and felt my own tears suddenly. Until that moment I hadn't told anyone I was scared, and now that I had, I was overwhelmed with relief.

He waited for me to collect myself, then he took my hands. Our fingers locked, and I took in a long deep breath.

"I want us to be together," he said finally.

"No, you don't."

"Yes, I do."

"You haven't given this any thought—the fact that it's not your child—the fact that there *is* a child." I took a deep breath. "And even if you did think about it and you did actually want to do it, there are other things we'd have to work out."

"I know."

I wondered if we were talking about the same thing.

"We're talking about the same thing," he said, as if he were reading my mind. "My shrink gave me a prescription for that."

"You switched off Prozac?"

"No." He looked at me. "He gave me a prescription for something else."

"Oh," I said. *"Oh."*

He ran his thumbs along my wrists, and then he tightened his grip on my hands.

"Does it work?" I asked.

"I don't know. I haven't tried it. Yet."

I smiled. "This is ridiculous."

"What's ridiculous?"

"Just when you can finally, you know—"

"Have sex?"

"I can't."

"What do you mean you can't?"

"Because I'm—"

"You can have sex while you're pregnant," he said.

"I know, but isn't it kind of dangerous?"

"Not if you do it right."

I looked at him. "How do you do it right?"

He touched the side of my face with his hand. "I'll show you," he said. "I'll show you."

And later that night, he did.

ACKNOWLEDGMENTS

For help, friendship, and advice, I am grateful to Bill Clegg, Julie Grau and her family, Nico Hartman, Ivan Held, Susan Kamil, Wendy Law-Yone, Julia Matheson, Nancy Pearlstein, and Elise and Lily Ana Supovitz. For devotion, heretofore unknown, Brendan Dealy.

ABOUT THE AUTHOR

Laura Zigman grew up in Newton-
ville, Massachusetts, and spent ten
years working in the book publishing
industry in New York. Her pieces have
appeared in *The New York Times, The
Washington Post,* and *USA Today.* She
lives in Washington, D.C.